FOREVER YOUR DUKE

ERICA RIDLEY

Never Say Duke

Dukes, Actually

The Duke's Bride

The Duke's Embrace

The Duke's Desire

Dawn With a Duke

One Night With a Duke

Ten Days With a Duke

Forever Your Duke

Gothic Love Stories:

Too Wicked to Kiss

Too Sinful to Deny

Too Tempting to Resist

Too Wanton to Wed

Too Brazen to Bite

Magic & Mayhem:

Kissed by Magic

Must Love Magic

Smitten by Magic

The *Wicked Dukes Club*:

One Night for Seduction by Erica Ridley

One Night of Surrender by Darcy Burke

One Night of Passion by Erica Ridley

One Night of Scandal by Darcy Burke

One Night to Remember by Erica Ridley

One Night of Temptation by Darcy Burke

ACKNOWLEDGMENTS

As always, I could not have written this book without the invaluable support of my critique partner, beta readers, and editors. Huge thanks go out to Erica Monroe and Tessa Shapcott. You are the best!

Lastly, I want to thank my *Historical Romance Book Club*, and my fabulous street team. Your enthusiasm makes the romance happen.

Thank you so much!

CRESSMOUTH GAZETTE

Welcome to Christmas!

Our picturesque village is nestled around Marlowe Castle, high atop the gorgeous mountain we call home. Cressmouth is best known for our year-round Yuletide cheer. Here, we're family.

The legend of our twelve dukes? Absolutely true! But they may not always be in the manner one might expect…

CHAPTER 1

December 1814

As her cousin's carriage rounded another hairpin turn up the snow-covered mountain, Miss Cynthia Louise Finch did her best to keep the playing cards and gambling chips from sliding off the squab in front of them.

Gertie flashed out an arm to block her puppy from tumbling off of the seat beside her. Her other hand gripped two playing cards tight enough to dent the stiff paper.

"Are two Jacks good enough?" she asked in a tiny, hesitant voice.

They had been playing *vingt-et-un* for the entire hour's ride north from Houville. So far, Gertie was afraid of winning, losing, and wagering.

"Two Jacks are wonderful," Cynthia Louise assured her cousin for the third time since she'd dealt the cards. "Remember, you're not supposed to let me *know* that you have two Jacks. I can see them from here, and even if I couldn't, you've dented the bottoms in such a way that I'll be able to recognize those cards as Jacks in all future deals."

Gertie lay the Jacks face-up on her primrose velvet pelisse and attempted to smooth the crinkles from the cards.

"Face-down," Cynthia whispered.

Gertie flipped the cards over. "You already knew I had two Jacks."

"I didn't know it was the Jack of Diamonds and Jack of Clubs," Cynthia pointed out.

Gertie looked horrified. "You didn't say suit mattered!"

"It *doesn't* matter in *vingt-et-un*," Cynthia tried to explain. "But if we were playing whist or—"

The terrified look in Gertie's eyes indicated she'd throw herself from the moving carriage before attempting something as complex and ruinous as whist.

"Try to remember," Cynthia said gently. "It's a good habit never to show your cards."

"It's hopeless. *I'm* hopeless." Gertie threw her wrinkled cards atop the deck and dropped her last remaining buttons onto the wagering pile in defeat. "How can Father expect me to win a duke if I can't even manage *vingt-et-un*?"

"You're a sweet, beautiful, well-bred young lady," Cynthia answered. "And if for some reason that isn't enough, you also have *me*. I am the wild card who will help you win Nottingvale's favor."

Gertie's delicate face lost some of its pallor, and she gave a tremulous smile. "You can do anything. That's why Father sent you with me."

2

This was partly true.

Cynthia liked to believe she *could* do almost anything—which was what made her a terrible choice in chaperone. She was more likely to play skittles at the Frost Fair as to stay home embroidering handkerchiefs.

According to anyone who had ever read a scandal column, Cynthia's irrepressible hoydenish ways were the reason she was destined to remain a spinster for the rest of her days.

To her uncle the earl, Cynthia's spinsterness was what recommended her most as chaperone. At the ungodly advanced age of thirty, *she* wouldn't be attracting the Duke of Nottingvale's romantic attentions.

Because she was the sole unmarried adult female in the extended family, Cynthia was also the only woman with no other responsibilities during the festive season.

As a native of the closest village to Cressmouth, Cynthia had attended the Duke of Nottingvale's annual Christmastide party for years.

This year, His Grace intended to select a bride from his Yuletide guests.

Cynthia's role was to make certain that bride was Gertie.

"But, Cynthia Louise..." Gertie whispered. "What if he hates me?"

"He won't hate you. No one hates you." Cynthia tucked the cards back into their box. "No one *knows* you, darling. You don't talk to anyone. You're going to have to speak to Nottingvale on occasion so that he notices you're there."

Gertie looked as though Cynthia had just suggested performing a naked trapeze act at the circus.

"I can't talk to him. I can't talk to anyone. I never know what to say." Gertie pulled Max onto her lap and gripped him tight. "Can't you do the talking for me? You always know what to do."

"I rarely know what to do," Cynthia corrected. "I just pick something and do it."

"*Yes*." Gertie's eyes shone as if Cynthia had just confessed to dark magic. "You weren't the least bit shy when you begged cousin Olaf to show you how to use his skis."

Cynthia scooped the gambling buttons back into their bag. "I'm not certain that skis—"

"You weren't timid at all when those fops challenged you to a bout of fencing," Gertie continued.

"You definitely shouldn't copy that," Cynthia said firmly. "Fops can be dangerous."

"And I've never seen anything so brave as the time you climbed up the tallest tree in Hyde Park to rescue a little girl's kite," Gertie finished dreamily. "I can't even climb a *small* tree."

"You're not supposed to climb trees," Cynthia reminded her cousin. "The duke's primary requirement is a proper young lady, and you're the properest young lady I know. That's your trump card."

Gertie frowned. "What's a trump card again?"

"Your advantage," Cynthia explained. "The thing that makes you better than all of the other choices."

"But I'm not better." Gertie's face was pale. "All of the young ladies will be well-mannered debutantes from good families, just like me. And they won't turn into a potato with all eyes and no mouth if the duke happens to glance in their direction."

"You'll be the prettiest potato the duke has ever seen," Cynthia assured her. "If you can't think of anything to say, nod and look interested. That will get you through more conversations than you might expect. It's how Barbara landed *her* husband."

Gertie brightened. "Barbara is very happy. You did a splendid job with both of my sisters."

Cynthia had become the de facto companion for her younger, prettier cousins after her sixth and final Season passed without a peep of interest from anyone. There hadn't even been a *bad* proposal to turn down.

She was glad of it. Who needed a husband?

With a high-in-the-instep duke like Nottingvale glowering down his patrician nose at her, there would be no trees or skis or skittles.

Cynthia was much happier as a spinster. Her life had become exponentially easier the moment she decided to abandon high society's stifling rules in favor of having none at all. Without having to worry about attracting potential suitors, she was free to live as she pleased.

She was never going back.

"Max, no!" Gertie scolded. "You'll muss my traveling dress!"

See? Cynthia didn't give two figs about wrinkled muslin. Being unmarriageable was so much better than trying to be presentable all of the time.

"I'll take him."

The puppy was already leaping from Gertie's

bodice to Cynthia's lap before she finished the sentence.

"He's impossible," Gertie said fondly. "You're *certain* the duke won't mind that we've brought him?"

"If he does, we'll say Max is my dog." Scrunching up her face, Cynthia tried not to laugh as the small, wiggly brown puppy licked her face exuberantly.

See? Canine saliva glistening on one's cheeks was no problem at all when one was an unmarriageable spinster.

"What if the duke *does* pick me?" Gertie said in horror. "Will I have to give up Max?"

"Of course not." Cynthia rubbed between his ears. "I'll 'give' Max back to you as an early wedding present. It would be rude of the duke not to accept a family member's wedding present, and the Duke of Nottingvale is never rude. He's always perfectly proper. It's in his blood."

"He frightens me," Gertie whispered. "He's so big."

"Well, he is tall," Cynthia admitted. "And those wide shoulders are difficult to miss. But try to concentrate on the other details. He has very long eyelashes for a duke. They're the same deep brown as his eyes. The left side of his mouth turns up a little more than the right when he smiles. That's a flaw, isn't it? One can barely tear one's gaze away. As for all of those trim muscles from boxing and swimming..."

Wait.

What was she supposed to be talking about?

Cynthia busied herself balancing Max upside-down on her lap in order to rub his soft belly and thereby avoid meeting her cousin's eyes.

Cynthia did not fancy the Duke of Nottingvale. She did *not*.

Gertie depended on Cynthia—the entire family depended upon her—and she was going to deliver. Nottingvale would be smitten with Gertie at first sight. This would be the easiest matchmaking mission of Cynthia's life.

She just had to survive a fortnight of other people's flirtations.

"Look!" Cynthia pointed out of the window at a bright red wooden sign rising from the snow.

Welcome to Christmas!

Gertie's eyes widened. "Is it really Christmastide here all year round?"

Unlike Cynthia, Gertie was not from the northernmost corner of England. Gertie and her family spent half of the year in London, and the other half near Southampton, where Gertie's father had a seaside manor.

"It really is," Cynthia said with a grin. "Marlowe Castle sits atop the highest point, overlooking the cheerful little village. Despite its small size, Cressmouth has dozens of entertainments at any moment. What happened to this month's timetable?"

"Here it is!" Gertie pulled a battered copy of the Cressmouth Gazette out from under Max's basket, and turned to the long lists of December activities beginning on page four.

Cynthia didn't need to review the newspaper to know what delights it contained. Accommodations in Cressmouth were expensive, but most of the entertainments were free. Since she lived only an hour's drive away—an hour and a half, perhaps, in snowy conditions such as these—Cynthia came up to spend the day whenever the Christmas spirit struck her.

In addition to being an absolute paradise for all things Yuletide, Cressmouth's coziness would be another advantage over the London season.

Cynthia hoped.

Gertie's come-out earlier that year had been a middling success.

Despite failing to mumble a shy response to any of her many smitten suitors, Gertie's dance card remained full and her father's mantel fairly sagged under the weight of so many calling cards.

None of the interested parties was good enough for the daughter of an earl, however. Gertie might not speak to strangers, but Lady Gertrude would be a disappointment to her family if she landed anything less than a wealthy aristocrat.

Cynthia knew exactly what it felt like to be a disappointment to one's family. Now she did it on purpose, but once upon a time she had tried to fit in and to be chosen.

It hadn't worked.

Her dance card, like the visitor dish upon her mantel, had remained empty.

Gertie, on the other hand, had a fighting

chance. Cynthia considered this a rescue mission as much as a matchmaking one. Despite Gertie being all of eighteen years old, her father was planning to betroth her to one of his ancient, lecherous peers as part of a political alliance. Gertie would be miserable.

Cynthia *liked* Nottingvale. Any woman would be lucky to have him.

Cynthia loved her cousin Gertie. She truly believed the duke wouldn't be able to help falling in love... if Cynthia could convince Gertie to speak in a voice loud enough to be heard, and to show the duke who she really was.

That was the best part of a Christmastide house party. Intimate close quarters where Nottingvale and Gertie would run into each other a dozen times a day. Even for shy Gertie, It would be impossible to avoid the duke.

"Here we are," Cynthia said briskly as the carriage pulled up in front of the duke's so-called cottage.

The only larger residence in Cressmouth was the castle itself.

Smart black carriages stretched down the long winding driveway up to Nottingvale's cheerful brick façade.

Exquisitely dressed young ladies stepped onto the shoveled path, accompanied by equally proper-looking matrons ranging from hired companions to marriage-minded mothers.

Cynthia recognized most of them. Not the debutantes—she'd been out of society far too long for that. Many of the older ladies had either been in London the same time Cynthia was, or lived near enough to this area that they'd crossed paths in Cressmouth before, perhaps even at one of Nottingvale's previous parties.

"Ready?" she murmured to Gertie.

Her cousin looked like she was going to be ill. "*No.*"

The carriage door swung open. A pair of gorgeously liveried footmen Cynthia recognized as Horace and Morris appeared at the opening to hand her and her cousin out of the coach.

"Pluck up, darling." She dug her elbow into Gertie's side. "You're the swan following the ugly duckling into the water. There's no need for speeches. You smile and curtsey and say 'How do you do?' just like we practiced."

"Can we practice some more?" Gertie whispered. "Maybe we should come back next year."

"He's picking a bride this year," Cynthia reminded her. "This is the only opportunity. If you're not inside that house when the Duke of Nottingvale…"

There he was.

Right there in the doorway.

He'd only been visible for a brief moment. Half in shadow behind his stoic butler Oswald, a shaft of sunlight had fallen onto the Duke of Nottingvale's absurdly handsome face and touchably tousled soft brown hair whilst he passed from one side of the entryway to another.

A second or two. The space of a heartbeat.

Cynthia's breath froze solid in her lungs. She had become as stiff and silent as an icicle, teetering precipitously before a fall.

"All right." Gertie's voice was brave as she

looped her arm trustingly through Cynthia's. "I can survive it with you at my side."

"Wonderful," Cynthia croaked. Absolutely marvelous. The moment they'd both been waiting for.

It was time to matchmake Nottingvale to her cousin.

CHAPTER 2

*H*is Grace Alexander Borland, seventh Duke of Nottingvale, stalked from room to room, ensuring everything was in order. The month-long Christmastide party was an annual tradition, and this year it had to be perfect.

It was already a disaster.

A sudden snowstorm had halted all travel for the past fortnight, reducing Alexander's party from four weeks to two. He himself had only arrived that morning, just in time to have a hurried meeting with business partners for a project they'd intended to complete *last* week, only for—

"Guests are arriving," announced Oswald, the butler.

There was no need to adjust postures. Oswald was perpetually stoic and ramrod-straight. Respectable and proper at all times, just as Alexander liked.

The butler opened the door and the first team of liveried footmen rushed out into the cold, ready to bring in heavy trunks and hand guests down from carriages with all of the elegance and efficiency they deserved.

But they weren't the first to arrive.

Alexander's new business partners, Calvin and Jonathan, were staying through the grand Twelfth Night gala. Alexander had no idea where they were at this moment, which was just as well, because he did not have time to make dozens of introductions on top of ensuring the perfection of every detail of his party.

The *almost* perfection.

As a consequence of the inconvenient snowstorm, the arrival of Alexander's mother, the Duchess of Nottingvale, was also delayed.

No gentleman could host a house party on his own. A hostess must always play the lead role. As an impeccably dignified matriarch, his mother was perfect for the part.

In the meantime, Alexander's younger sister Lady Isabelle would have to do.

Belle was... no longer completely respectable.

While Alexander had spent the past fortnight burrowing north from London to distant Cressmouth, his sister Belle had apparently spent the past weeks in the arms of Alexander's business partner Calvin, resulting in their betrothal.

Alexander's surprise at his sister's impending marriage to a tailor would be nothing compared to the duchess's reaction once Mother arrived.

Belle had fallen in love, not that romance would sway the matriarch's opinion.

Alexander was dependable. He had never been in love, nor would he allow emotion to overtake him. A duke was logical, unemotional, and above all things: proper.

There were *rules*.

Alexander followed them.

Strict adherence to expectations and station was the only way to ensure one's life unfolded with clockwork precision.

"Any further instructions, Your Grace?" asked a footman.

"Be ready," Alexander replied.

The kitchen had been instructed to avoid strawberries, due to one of the guests' adverse reactions to the fruit. The maids had replaced another guest's feather pillows with soft wool stuffing, once Alexander learned downy feathers made her sneeze. He kept detailed notes so that returning guests' experiences would be even better than the previous year.

He didn't want his party to be *good*.

He needed it to be *flawless*.

This was the day before Christmas Eve. His friends were entrusting Alexander with their Yuletide. He wanted them all to have the best holiday possible.

"Here they come, Your Grace," said the butler.

Alexander's sister Belle joined him in greeting the guests.

He positioned himself a respectable distance from the open door and greeted each guest as they entered the cottage, before handing them off to a footman or maid to show them to their guest chambers.

Alexander had assigned rooms with the same care he devoted to every aspect of his life. Windows with morning light for the early risers. Snorers grouped as far as possible from light sleepers. Extra blankets and fully stocked fireplaces for everyone.

Locals began to fill the parlor as well, partaking of the strawberry-less refreshments and chatting with old friends they hadn't seen since Alexander's previous Christmastide party.

At a break in the tide, he turned to his sister. "As soon as Mother arrives, you can relax."

"*Can* I?" she said doubtfully, but her eyes twinkled with merriment.

Excellent point.

"As soon as Mother arrives, you can hide," he corrected. "I've given you and Calvin adjoining rooms on the opposite side of the house as hers. This is your Yuletide, too. I want you to enjoy it."

She gave him an arch look. "Will *you* enjoy it?"

"It's not my duty to make merry," he reminded her firmly. "It's my duty to ensure everyone else does."

She didn't look convinced. "When was the last time you enjoyed anything, even when other people's happiness wasn't riding on the outcome?"

"It's not my purpose to—"

"You're a *duke*, not a gear in a pocket watch. You can change the pace once in a while. Not everything has to be controlled down to the second."

It was Alexander's turn to look appalled.

Belle burst out laughing. "I suppose that snowstorm had you in a tizzy."

"Dukes don't tizzy," he informed her.

"Mm-hm. You probably stalked out-of-doors

and commanded the snow to stop falling in that imperious all-things-must-go-according-to-plan way you have."

He lifted a shoulder. "It stopped snowing, did it not?"

"I'm surprised you didn't pull your hair out in panic." She tilted her head. "Never mind. You would never allow a hair on your head to be out of place, no matter the wind's wishes. You'd command the clouds if you could."

"You're hilarious," he told her. "No one has ever had a wittier sister. Your jests warm my heart."

"You don't let anything near your heart," she said. "You're too busy being perfect to enjoy your own parties. You could be replaced with an automaton and I'd be the only one to notice."

That was hardly fair.

"You used to be straitlaced too," he reminded her.

"And look how much better my life is now," Belle shot back. "Particularly compared to yours." She crooked her elbows at ninety-degree angles and made stiff, choppy motions whilst speaking in monotone. "'I am a clockwork duke. Tick tock, I love rules.'"

Alexander lifted his nose.

Life would be easier if *everyone* followed rules.

He was grateful to have them. Rules let him know what to do and what to expect. Rules were what guided him when he'd inherited the title as an adolescent. He'd felt lost without his father, but the rules had given him a path to follow to succeed.

What Alexander wanted to do didn't signify in

the least. A duke did what must be done, and refrained from all activities not befitting his station.

Especially a respectable duke on the hunt for an equally proper bride.

He was glad that his sister had found love, but there would be scandal when the gossips heard the news. Any latitude Alexander might have had before was now gone. It was up to him to salvage the family's reputation.

With luck, it would all be over soon.

He and Belle turned back to the doorway as a new wave of guests splashed inside.

This would be the biggest crush yet. With Alexander's permission, his mother had let it be known that her son was finally seeking a duchess.

Hopeful young misses flooded his cottage. They might be in competition with each other, but Alexander knew his own behavior was now under a microscope as well.

Not only did mothers and chaperones want their charges to make a splendid match... Those spurned would be happy to spread gossip of any of the duke's faults.

His duty was not to have any.

He *and* his party must be perfect.

"Of course," his sister assured a highly respected society matron, all traces of her earlier irreverence gone. "I would be honored to show you and your daughter to your chambers. Follow me, please."

Alexander was glad for Belle's presence.

She was a meddlesome sister, but a wonderful hostess. For all her teasing, she would help ensure no unwelcome surprises happened to—

Miss Cynthia Louise Finch stood on his front step, holding a mongrel puppy aloft to his impressively stoic butler.

His heart stopped, then raced faster.

Miss Finch was the opposite of proper.

She was a firework in a box of candles.

Everything about her was significantly more than necessary. She had two names when one would suffice. She brought a dog to a house party. She was tall, with abundant curves. She had apple cheeks and plump rosy lips and big blue eyes.

Her excessiveness ought to be overwhelming, but instead made him feel as though he stood dizzyingly close to a statue of a Grecian goddess come to life.

"Is that a dog?" called out one of the locals.

"It *is*. Meet Max!" She swept into the room brandishing the wiggling puppy in front of her chest, passing the mongrel off to the first taker.

It was not at all how a proper young lady would enter the home of a duke—or anywhere.

It was *not done*.

Which made it classic Cynthia Louise Finch.

"Who wants to go ice racing later?" she asked her friends at the refreshment table.

"Do you mean ice *skating*?" asked one.

"She means ice *racing*," said another. "I lost ten quid to her last December."

Miss Finch laughed in delight. "Want to lose another ten?"

Had the audacious hoyden failed to notice his receiving party of one?

He hoped she hadn't glimpsed the Duke of Nottingvale ducking ignominiously into the closest shadow rather than greet Miss Cynthia Louise without the protective buffer of his sister at his side.

Belle was the reason Miss Finch was here.

Belle had been bashful during her come-out. Her first season had not gone as planned. At the time, Miss Finch was on her sixth unsuccessful season. She'd been extraordinarily kind to Belle, and earned a lifelong friend in the process.

And by extension, an open invitation to Alexander's famous Christmastide house parties. How he had railed against the suggestion!

Alexander had been certain Miss Finch would not get on with any of his guests.

He had been wrong.

She lived an hour away in Houville. Miss Finch visited Cressmouth so often, she'd been on a first-name basis with every soul in the village long before Alexander ever built his cottage.

She might have fizzled out of Polite Society after six years, but here in Cressmouth, she was celebrated like family.

He watched in horror.

Whilst her puppy was humping the leg to Alexander's refreshment table, Miss Finch linked arms with her cousin, a terrified-looking waif of eighteen years, and began introducing the chit to everyone in sight.

No amount of shadow could save him now.

It was only a matter of time before Miss Finch started toward Alexander.

His muscles tightened. The last thing he needed at a party as important as this was a dare-devil spinster causing trouble.

Alexander was in search of an aristocratic young lady who would bring honor and continued decorum to the esteemed Nottingvale dukedom.

Miss Finch's only connection to the aristocracy was an aunt who had married a second son, who decades later inherited an earldom. The waif at her side was the earl's youngest daughter, Lady Gertrude, whose come-out had occurred scant months earlier.

Miss Finch's come-out had been twelve long years ago. She'd had no dowry, no connections, and no luck. By society's standards, now she was simply *old*.

Yet it was difficult to think of Miss Finch as "on the shelf" when she never stood still.

Her brand of beauty was like a summer storm rising over the horizon. Fascinating to watch from a safe distance, but dangerous to go anywhere near.

And she was coming toward him.

"*There* you are," Miss Finch said as though Alexander had been hiding from her, which he absolutely had been. "Lady Gertrude, this is His Grace, the Duke of Nottingvale."

Despite the obvious terror on her face, Lady Gertrude dipped in an exquisite curtsey.

Alexander made an extravagant leg in response. "How do you do?"

Lady Gertrude swung panicked eyes toward Miss Finch.

"She's fine, thank you," Miss Finch said with good cheer, as though her mongrel were not currently climbing up the silk stocking of Alexander's footman. "We're both fine. Gertie made the journey up from London before the snow fell, and we've spent the past fortnight in Houville having a brilliant time of it. Haven't we, Gertie?"

Lady Gertrude's eyes grew even wider, her face worryingly pale.

"The carriage ride was quick enough," Miss Finch continued, "and your refreshment table as outstanding as I remembered. Why should drinking chocolate only be served at breakfast, I always say. Gertie loves chocolate, don't you, Gertie?"

Lady Gertrude blanched further.

"She is also an accomplished pianist, capable of the finest embroidery I have ever seen, and is well-versed in the minute details of managing the staff of a large estate. Now that her elder sisters have married, Gertie frequently steers the household of the country pile whilst her parents are in London. Don't let her young age fool you. If I had a dukedom, I would feel absolutely confident with Lady Gertrude at the helm."

"If you had a..." What the devil was Miss Finch talking about?

Dukedoms. *His* dukedom.

Lady Gertrude.

Miss Finch was *matchmaking*. Or at least, attempting to, her charge's frozen demeanor notwithstanding.

Alexander cleared his throat. "She certainly sounds..."

What was he doing, talking about Lady Gertrude in third person as though she weren't standing right in front of him?

He turned to Lady Gertrude and smiled.

She looked like a puff of air could knock her over.

"You certainly sound like a capable young lady." Capable of disappearing through the floorboards before allowing her eyes to meet his. "I look forward to speaking more with you—" Or hearing her speak at all, rather. "—over the course of the party."

There.

That was polite *and* true, and more than welcoming. Surely he could now extricate himself from Miss Finch's radiating energy, and slip off to—

A tiny bark sounded from beneath the biscuit table. A blur of brown fur shot out from under the tablecloth, only to launch itself up through the air in the direction of Alexander's freshly pressed and starched cravat.

Lady Gertrude's arms flashed out, snatching the puppy from thin air with lightning reflexes, only to toss the mongrel up over her shoulder in the direction of Miss Finch.

Miss Finch not only intercepted the puppy smoothly, as though this were a maneuver they'd practiced for months, she rubbed between his ears and continued talking as if nothing at all had occurred.

"Gertie is very organized," she was saying. "You have never seen a more orderly kitchen or library than the ones on the earl's estate. The household is gallingly neat. If you leave her alone too long near your refreshment table, you'll return to find every item in alphabetical order."

"It's already in alphabetical order," Alexander said.

He wasn't thinking about the refreshment table *or* Lady Gertrude.

The puppy had flopped belly-up against Miss Finch's bodice, all four paws with their tiny little pads pointing in four different directions. Alexander could swear the mongrel smiled as Miss Finch rubbed its belly, his little pink tongue hanging from his mouth in obvious ecstasy. His fur looked ridiculously soft.

Miss Finch lifted her arms in Alexander's direction. "Want to touch?"

He was now looking at her bare arms instead of the puppy.

Of course he was.

Alexander's footmen relieved guests of their winter hats and coats as they entered the cottage. It should not surprise him at all to discover Miss Finch clothed in a highly impractical lightweight frock with short puffed sleeves rather than the more sensible long-sleeved velvet-and-sarcenet of her young charge's gown.

Miss Finch's bare arms were completely exposed to the air... and to Alexander's gaze.

Her skin looked just as soft as the puppy snuggling into her arms. Soft and warm, for there was no sign of gooseflesh upon her skin.

Until she noticed him looking. Goosebumps rippled down her arm as a flush raced up her cheeks.

Alexander's own neck was uncomfortably warm as he broke his gaze and began mumbling incoherently.

"A basket," he said. "It'll be sent to your room at once. And a small blanket to put in the basket. And a bowl of water. And a bone—"

At the word *bone*, the puppy leapt from Miss Finch's arms and darted off through the well-dressed crowd.

Lady Gertrude vanished after him, with Miss Finch right on her heels, leaving Alexander babbling about his supply of bones to the empty air.

He closed his mouth with a click just as Oswald swung the front door back open.

Her Grace, the Duchess of Nottingvale swept into the cottage.

"Thank God," Alexander said.

His mother exuded proper decorum from every pore. Her presence would ensure respectable comportment by all parties.

"Oh, Vale," she said as they exchanged cheek kisses. "How I apologize for the horrid delay."

"Perfectly understandable," he assured her. "I arrived this morning, and we're still missing half of the guests."

Three-eighths of the guests, to be exact. He'd been checking them off in his head as they crossed the threshold.

"And your sister?" his mother asked. "I presume she's been an exemplary hostess in my stead."

"Yes," he replied without elaborating.

There would be plenty of time later for *and she had a torrid affair with my tailor, to whom she's now betrothed.*

Much, much later.

At least, he *hoped* there was time to find a bride

and prove himself utterly above reproach before the scandal sheets tore his family apart.

Mother would be appalled when she learned Belle had prioritized love over her reputation. Mother was the one who had taught Alexander the trick of following society's rules, no matter what. It was how she had learned to be a duchess, and how he had learned to be a duke.

Entire books had been written on proper comportment, and Alexander had memorized every one. He expected no less from his future duchess.

Mother surveyed the growing crowd. "I suppose you think a fortnight won't be long enough."

Yes. That was exactly what he thought.

It was like having to select the right goldfish from a fishbowl of identical goldfish. There was nothing wrong with *any* of the goldfish, which wasn't the point at all. A duke was meant to select the *best*.

Somehow.

By observing two dozen polite, pretty debutantes in an unnatural environment over the course of fourteen days.

"It'll be easy," Mother assured him. "You'll know by Epiphany."

He certainly prayed for an epiphany.

"They know I intend to announce the betrothal at the Twelfth Night gala?"

"Yes. Choosing your young lady for the first dance will make a lovely statement," Mother agreed. "She can spend the rest of the ball by your side, as your hostess. Have you anyone in mind?"

"The first carriage just arrived an hour ago."

"Plenty of time to whittle down the choices."

Mother narrowed her eyes at the milling crowd. "The Twittington girl is slouching. You don't want a slouchy duchess. The Whittleburr chit won't stop twirling her hair. I absolutely cannot abide a hair-twirler at the dinner table. And that one over there..." Mother frowned. "Who is she?"

He turned to look. "That's Lady Gertrude."

"Excellent posture," Mother said, impressed. "She's neither twirling her hair, nor running on at the mouth like some of these vapid chatterboxes."

No, Lady Gertrude did not seem the sort to talk a man's ear off.

"We'll see," said the duchess. "Whomever you choose—"

"—must be a credit to the title," he finished. "I know my duty."

Alexander had many privileges, but a love match was not one of them. He had a dukedom to consider. A family, whose reputations would be impacted by his choice. Heirs of his own one day, who should be afforded every advantage Alexander could provide.

If having a sister had taught him anything, it was that women could be as strong and as stubborn as any man... and just as scandalous. Alexander had to take great care.

He needed a nice, safe, sweet, *predictable* bride. A wife he need never worry about, because she would always do the right thing.

"Who is Lady Gertrude *with?*" asked his mother. "Good heavens! Please tell me the poor dear's 'chaperone' isn't Miss Cynthia Louise Finch."

"For the next fortnight," he answered bleakly.

Or weakly.

He was looking at Miss Finch's bare arms again and trying not to wonder what her skin would feel like beneath his fingertips.

All he had to do was avoid her.

It shouldn't be a difficult task. Miss Finch had a long history of sneaking off from his party after Christmas Day to take part in the village's many festive activities. She appeared to believe no one ever noticed her sly absences.

Mayhap no one did.

No one except Alexander.

He was *glad* she was such a rude guest. Her disinterest in his company was a boon to them both.

While she was ice-racing or setting off fireworks from the castle turrets, he would be right here selecting the perfect future duchess.

CHAPTER 3

ynthia Louise placed a gentle hand on her younger cousin's heaving back. *"Breathe."*

"I can't," came Gertie's muffled voice between shuddering breaths. She lifted her wan face from the shallow burlap bag she'd been breathing into. "Cynthia Louise, I *can't* go caroling."

"You know all of the words," Cynthia reminded her. "You know the songs so well, you could play them at the pianoforte blindfolded. Besides, it's not a solo. We'll be in a large group—"

"That's it," said Gertie desperately. "I'll stay here playing the pianoforte whilst everyone else goes door-to-door, *singing*. Out loud. In front of people."

"We can stand in the back," Cynthia promised. "You can mouth the words. No one will know."

Gertie clutched the burlap bag to her chest. "If no one will notice, why must we go?"

"Nottingvale can't choose you if he never *sees* you." Cynthia knelt beside the four-poster bed. "You've been in this guest chamber all day. You missed breakfast—"

"I rang for service," Gertie mumbled. "He has good chocolate."

"—and you missed luncheon—"

"I had that delivered as well. They were very nice sandwiches. I sent a note of appreciation back to the kitchen."

"It's Christmas Eve, darling. We're at a Christmastide party. In a village called Christmas." Cynthia took the battered bag from Gertie's hands and placed it on the bedside table. "Come and be festive, just for a few hours."

"You promise I'll like it?" came Gertie's timid voice.

"No," Cynthia answered honestly. "But I promise you will survive it. I'll be there, too. And we can take Max."

Gertie brightened. "All right. I'll go if Max goes."

"That's the right outlook, darling."

Was it a good outlook? Cynthia had her doubts. But at this point, she'd be willing to strap antlers to Max's head and pretend he was a reindeer if that was what it took to coax Gertie back to the party.

The plan had seemed simple enough on the carriage ride up.

The duke was in search of a bride.

Point him toward Lady Gertrude.

This plan presupposed that Gertie and the duke would occasionally occupy the same room at the same time. Worse, while Gertie burrowed her head in a burlap sack, the rest of the debutantes threw themselves at Nottingvale.

Even worse, every single one of them was... a true delight.

As near as Cynthia could tell, Nottingvale could close his eyes and pick a bride at random, and end up with a pretty, well mannered, respectable young lady worthy of the title of duchess, no matter which contender he chose.

The key was to have Gertie within sight when Nottingvale pointed his finger.

"Come along," Cynthia said briskly. "Shall we choose an unwrinkled gown?"

"Why?" Gertie asked suspiciously. "Won't we be bundled in coats and capes?"

Cynthia unfolded a fresh gown. "We'll be meeting in the parlor for biscuits and wassail prior to heading out in the cold."

Gertie looked as though she'd rather hide under the bed with Max.

"You *like* biscuits and wassail," Cynthia reminded her.

"I could ring for it," Gertie said hopefully. "We could consume ours in here."

Cynthia held out the new dress.

With a resigned huff, Gertie slid out of the tall bed and trudged over to don the fresh gown.

"I'm going to drink all of the wassail," she warned. "They'll have to refill the bowl five times, because I'm going to drink until I warble carols like an opera singer on opening night."

"At least Nottingvale would notice you." Cynthia arched a brow. "If you're waiting for me to talk you out of a hilariously muttonheaded idea, you're speaking to the wrong cousin. I could come up with a lively dance to accompany your rousing choruses."

"Then he'd notice *you*," Gertie muttered. Her eyes widened. "Can you pretend to be me? Maybe we can switch at the altar if I wear a heavy enough veil."

Gooseflesh danced along Cynthia's arms at the remembrance of that brief moment the night before when the Duke of Nottingvale *had* seemed to notice her.

She still wasn't certain what to make of it. Or how to forget it.

"No switching at the altar," she said firmly. "His Grace knows who I am. More importantly, you need to come to know each other. I won't have you frightened of him on your wedding day. What will the guests think of you gasping into a burlap bag beneath your pretty veil?"

"I won't know," Gertie said. "I won't be able to see the witnesses because my face will be buried inside a burlap bag. Can we take it caroling with us?"

"Max comes. The bag stays." Cynthia hauled her cousin to the doorway.

"Come on, Max," Gertie cooed. "Here, boy."

The little brown puppy crawled out from under the bed and leapt into Gertie's arms.

Cynthia tapped her heavy reticule to ensure Max's coiled leash was inside, then steered her cousin down the corridor toward the sounds of laughter and revelry.

"—caroling," the Duke of Nottingvale was saying, "followed by additional refreshments and dancing when we return."

A cheer rose up all around him.

Despite the crowded parlor, Cynthia could make Nottingvale out perfectly. She was tall and he was tall, which meant their startled eyes could meet over the tops of the heads of most of the guests.

She tried to glance away, but could not.

It had always been like that with Nottingvale. Or Vale, as his friends called him—which did not include Cynthia Louise Finch. She was tolerated at his Christmastide parties for the same reason her calendar hadn't been completely bare during her six failed London seasons.

She had just enough social connections not to be given the cut direct.

And not enough of anything else to bother inviting to the dance floor.

Cynthia wondered if her come-out had set a nationwide record. Six years of nightly fêtes, soirées, dinner parties, and grand galas... with nary a single dance.

It had been interminable.

The subsequent six years were much better. Not because aristocrats like Nottingvale suddenly deigned to dance with her—*Ha!*—but because Cynthia had stopped trying to impress people who had already decided they weren't interested.

Cressmouth's celebrated Marlowe Castle hosted open balls all year long. Cynthia danced until her feet hurt with the local blacksmith, the local baker, the local dairy farmer, the local solicitor, the local wine smuggler, the local parson...

They'd all married different women, but they hadn't looked through her as though she were less substantial than fog. They were *friends*, which was more than she'd had in London.

Here in Cressmouth, she now had three god-children, all of whom called her "Aunt Cynthia Louise" with varying abilities to pronounce the complicated letters, making it the cutest thing any spinster had ever heard.

Who cared if she was still invisible to the beau monde? She had her own world. One in which she mattered, and was seen.

Kind of like the way the Duke of Nottingvale was staring at her at this moment.

His warm brown eyes sent a glow of heat over her skin, as though she'd wandered too near the fireplace.

The duke hadn't had a moment to himself since the morning began, which somehow made him all the more attractive. His rumpled brown hair looked touchably soft, his jawline just as touchably rough. The hint of shadow instead of his usual close-shaved perfection made him seem... approachable. More real. Less regal.

He would be horrified if he knew.

"What is he looking at?" came a whisper from behind.

"Get up there," hissed another woman. "Fall into step with him while he's distracted, and don't leave his side until he's forced to ask you to tonight's first dance."

"But the dancing isn't for hours, Mama," came a panicked whisper that reminded Cynthia of Gertie. "What am I supposed to talk about?"

Eighteen years was far too young to make decisions that would impact one's future forevermore. Cynthia wished all of these desperate debutantes had a few years to find out who they were before they were forced to find a husband.

"Dukes don't want wives who *talk*," snapped the mother. "Sing the carols and look pretty. You don't want to end up a thirty-year-old spinster with no prospects, do you?"

Cynthia blinked.

A *thirty*-year-old spinster with no prospects. That was oddly specific.

"Your Hortense is nothing like Miss Finch," scolded another mother. "Our daughters are well-behaved and *pretty*."

Gertie stiffened and slowly lifted Max away from her bodice.

"Do not throw your puppy in her face," Cynthia whispered. "Even if she deserves it."

"We're *right here*," Gertie whispered back. "We're not invisible."

Ah. This was her first time.

Gertie had never been invisible. That was a large cause of her anxiety. She was used to people staring at her everywhere she went.

"I'm an 'ape leader,'" Cynthia reminded her. "I don't care."

"I hate that term," Gertie said fiercely. "Why are unwed dukes *more* eligible as they get older, and women less eligible by the day? It's not fair!"

"Lesson number one," Cynthia murmured. "Nothing is fair."

Gertie's eyes flashed. "They talk about you like you're a... a *cautionary tale*."

"I prefer 'folk legend.' You recall this past February when the river Thames froze over and I helped an elephant to cross the ice? Jolly good fun!" Cynthia wiggled her eyebrows. "Proper matrons *dream* of amusing themselves half as well as thirty-year-old spinsters with no prospects. I enjoy being me."

It had taken catastrophic failure in the Marriage Mart for Cynthia to realize being a wife was like losing at whist. You played the game and lived with the consequences. It was about stratagems, not soulmates.

Love was an illusion. None of the young ladies in this room wanted to marry Nottingvale because they *liked* him. They wanted his money, his title, his status, his security. Those were the cards on the table.

In turn, he won a pretty bauble. A malleable, impressionable, unobjectionable young lady capable of being molded into the finest duchess England had ever seen.

Huzzah! A winning hand for all.

Unless you wanted *more*.

"Maybe I should be a spinster like you," Gertie said. "Would I make a good ape leader?"

Oh no.

"You cannot *decide* to be an ape leader," Cynthia whispered. "That's as bad as deciding to take the first churl who offers marriage, just because he asked."

"Nottingvale will be the first to offer," said Gertie. "If he asks."

"Nottingvale is not a churl," Cynthia said firmly. "He has all of the material things any woman in search of a secure future could possibly want, and..."

Gertie's eyes widened. "And?"

And I like him.

It would not do.

"He's clever," Cynthia forced herself to continue. "I've heard him debate with other gentlemen. He's honest to a fault. We all know why we're here. He's kind. He cares about all of his friends, even the local ones who've never stepped foot in Almack's assembly rooms. He's a dreadful singer."

Gertie blinked. "That's a good quality?"

"A wonderful quality. He doesn't let it stop him from enjoying Christmas. Don't let your shyness stop *you.*"

Gertie gazed doubtfully about the crowded room, then visibly straightened her spine.

"All right." She drew in a deep, shaky breath. "I'll take him."

There.

Cynthia got what she wanted.

She should be over the moon.

Gertie's mother had been Cynthia's sponsor all those years ago. The countess had arranged invitation after invitation, year after year, her faith in Cynthia never flagging.

Although the effort hadn't borne fruit, Cynthia would never forget what it had felt like to be believed in, fully and unconditionally. The countess was the reason Cynthia had started to believe in herself, despite all evidence that no one else did. The countess was the reason Cynthia wasn't afraid anymore. The reason Cynthia was happy.

And the countess was no longer with them.

Gertie's mother wasn't here to work the same

magic on her anxious daughter as she'd done for a shy and anxious Cynthia over a decade ago.

It was Cynthia's turn now.

She'd steered Gertie's older sisters into secure, *happy* marriages, and she would do the same for Gertie.

It was Cynthia's only hope to pay back her aunt for not treating her orphan niece as an object to be pitied, but rather as though Cynthia had been her daughter, too.

Worthy of her time.

Worthy of being loved.

This was Cynthia's chance to finally make the countess proud.

"Follow me, please!"

The Duchess of Nottingvale led the crowd past the gauntlet of footmen handing out hats and coats, and out into the snow-dazzled countryside like the Pied Piper of Yuletide Utopia.

Nottingvale adored his family. That was yet another mark in his favor.

Or another hurdle to cross.

"Why do I feel like she'll be harder to impress than the duke?" Gertie whispered.

"Because you're right," Cynthia said dryly. "Go on. Make a good impression."

Gertie bit her lip as she handed Max to Cynthia. "What do I do?"

"Be yourself. You're wonderful just as you are." Cynthia connected the leash to Max's collar. "And perhaps a compliment or two wouldn't go amiss."

"You should've let me bring my breathing sack," Gertie hissed, but she inched forward to blend with the debutantes.

By the fifth house, it was clear that every resident in Cressmouth had prepared vats of wassail to ladle out to carolers. Cynthia began to worry her cousin might make good on her threat to warble drunkenly into the night.

She tried to edge forward, but it was no use. Cynthia was stuck at the back of the crowd. Even her unusual height didn't help her with all of the top hats and feathered bonnets blocking the view.

"You're not singing," came a low voice on her left side.

She rose on her toes. "I'm waiting for 'A Spinster Goes A-Wenching.'"

A beat of silence.

"Isn't it 'A Soldier Goes A-Wenching?'"

"I changed the words. And the roles. What better buffet can there be for a self-respecting unwed wench than an entire squadron full of fit, handsomely uniformed—" Cynthia's heels came back to earth as she swung her gaze to her side in dawning suspicion.

No. It couldn't be.

Of course it was.

The Duke of Nottingvale smiled. "You were saying?"

"Dukes are fine, too?" she offered. "After one runs out of soldiers?"

"Flattering," he murmured. "For the soldiers."

The crowd began to move again.

Cynthia hung back and watched until she glimpsed Gertie up ahead with a remarkably sober gait and no signs of impending soprano solos.

Nottingvale hung back with her.

"Why aren't you up front and in the center?" Cynthia demanded.

There was that quick, crooked smile again. "Have you heard my singing voice?"

Fair point.

His grin widened. "I rest my case."

"It's not the *worst* singing voice," she hedged.

He hummed the first few bars of *A Soldier Goes A-Wenching*.

She clapped her mittens to the sides of her head. "My ears... Should they be bleeding like this?"

His dark eyes were curious. "You have a strange way of flirting."

"I'm not *flirting* with you," she said, aghast. "I'm an—" *Ape leader*. "—a chaperone. I want you to marry my cousin, the tremendously respectable Lady Gertrude."

"Whilst you go wenching amongst the soldiers?"

"Yes. Exactly."

He chuckled.

What was happening? None of this was right.

They were yards behind the rest of the group, who appeared to be singing merrily about Wenceslas, rather than wenching.

The duke's eyes were on her, not his guests. "I didn't send you that first invitation until my sister forced my hand."

"Yes," Cynthia said. "How thoughtful of you to point out my lack of welcome."

"The oversight was foolish of me." His lips twisted in self-deprecation. "You should write a ditty about that."

"I've written plenty of inappropriate ditties about you," she assured him, and immediately wished she hadn't.

He was too close.

A few tendrils of wavy brown hair curled out from under his top hat. The faint stubble along his chiseled jaw was *right there*, the sharp folds of his cravat pointing straight at it, as if daring her to brush her thumb against his rough skin and feel his warmth for herself.

She kept her thumbs tucked safely inside her mittens.

A gust of cold air whipped through the evergreens. She turned her face toward it, allowing the wind to flutter her bonnet as a distraction.

"Here," he said. "Let me help."

"No," she whispered, or *would* have whispered, if she had any power to make words at all.

The sound that escaped her throat sounded more like the whimper of a kitten.

He loosened the ribbon about her chin and set about retying it, his face an adorable mask of concentration as his knuckles grazed her cheek and neck.

He wasn't *really* touching her. He was wearing gloves. Touching did not count unless it was skin-to-skin, like, say, *kissing*, which she was not fantasizing breathlessly about *at all*.

"There," he said. "How is your dog doing?"

Dog? Cynthia didn't have a…

"*Max*," she gasped.

The puppy yipped and darted forward, pulling on the leash.

"I have to go," she said. "I'm busy—"

"—caroling," he supplied. "With the rest of us."

"Yes. Very busy. You should marry my cousin. Come along, Max. Gertie needs us."

Gertie was on a front step, accepting a fresh mug of steaming wassail from another happy Cressmouth resident.

Cynthia bowled through the crowd like a skittle-ball knocking down all ten pins at once.

"Wassail," she said to the cobbler's wife. "Please."

Cynthia handed Gertie Max's leash in order to wrap both mittens around the warm ceramic mug.

Gertie tilted her head. "Perhaps you'd make a better match with him than I would."

"What? No! Why would you—" Cynthia took a long gulp of wassail, which was much hotter than she expected it to be, leading to noises not unlike a cat coughing up a hair ball.

Cynthia's family were the only people who took her seriously.

They trusted her with Gertie, and Gertie's future.

Cynthia could not let them down.

"Nottingvale and I do not suit," she said firmly. "He's looking for someone like you. You happen to be *exactly* like you. It's a match made in heaven."

"All of the other young ladies are just like me, too."

"But they're *not* you," Cynthia pointed out. "That's their fatal flaw."

Gertie wrinkled her pert nose. "That's something someone who loves me would say."

Cynthia couldn't think of an appropriate rebuttal to that logic.

"Make certain no one else is his match first," Gertie said.

"*What?*"

"If you can promise me that the duke and I are *objectively* the best suited of everyone else here, then I..." Gertie picked up Max and cuddled him to her chest. "Then I'll promise to do whatever you say to win him."

Cynthia stared at her cousin. "What scale are we using? Imperial? Metric? How am I supposed to objectively ascertain the duke's compatibility with two dozen other women?"

Gertie lifted a shoulder. "Help him try."

Of all the...

"You want me to purposely attempt to match-make the duke to everyone else at the party, in the hopes that I fail, leaving him no choice but to choose you?"

Gertie nodded. "You're the best matchmaker in England. My sisters are *very* happy. You'll only be able to matchmake him to the person who's meant to be his bride."

"It better be you," Cynthia warned. "If he hasn't made his selection by Twelfth Night, I'm tossing you straight into his lap. If we return home without your betrothal to Nottingvale, your father will force you to marry that dreadful crusty viscount."

"You won't let that happen," Gertie said confidently. "You'll eliminate all of the others before Twelfth Night, thereby proving to me, Nottingvale, *and* our respective parents that ours is a perfect match."

Cynthia narrowed her eyes. "Is this an elaborate trick to stall for time, whilst you spend the next eleven days hiding in your bed with pots of hot chocolate and a burlap sack?"

"Yes." Gertie nuzzled between Max's ears. "No reneges."

"'No reneges' was for card games!" Cynthia grasped her cousin's arms. "You cannot renege, either. There's no hiding in bed whilst I do this. You have to take part in the planned activities so that Nottingvale has an opportunity to fall in love with you. If you don't..."

"I know." The color drained from Gertie's face and her breath grew uneven. "Father will trade me for a plot of land."

CHAPTER 4

The first grand ball to launch Alexander's annual Christmastide festivities was not off to a roaring start. Or even a lightly melodious start.

He had hired two talented brothers from London to provide musical accompaniment at the pianoforte for the duration of the party, but the gentlemen had been delayed first by snow, and now by a bout of influenza.

The bench at the pianoforte sat empty.

Guests milled about the perimeter of the room, chatting and sipping wine, and casting occasional glances at the freshly buffed and conspicuously unoccupied dance floor.

Alexander turned to ensure the refreshment table was freshly stocked.

Miss Finch stepped into his path with her cousin Lady Gertrude held captive by one arm.

"Is the dancing about to begin?" asked Miss Finch.

"No." Alexander sighed. "We haven't a pianist."

Miss Finch sent a dubious glance about the

crowded ballroom. "All of these highly accomplished ladies, and not one of them can play the pianoforte?"

"I'm certain they are all competent musicians," Alexander said quickly. He had no idea if this was true, but *she* seemed certain enough for the both of them. "But they are also guests who came here to dance. I cannot ask them to—"

"I'll do it." Lady Gertrude jerked her interlocked arm free from her cousin's.

Miss Finch looked alarmed. "Gertie, *no*. You're to have the first—"

But Lady Gertrude was half sprinting, half sliding across the freshly waxed floor. Her fingers were on the ivory keys even before her derrière touched the wooden bench.

The first notes of a popular country dance burst jauntily from the pianoforte.

In seconds, delighted guests clogged the dance floor, their lively patterns obstructing Lady Gertrude from view altogether.

"Thank you," Alexander said, and meant it. "You two have saved the party."

"Nothing so noble." Miss Finch sent a dark glance across the dance floor. "Lady Gertrude was saving herself."

"She's very talented."

The blithe compliment had been automatic, but when he paused to really listen, Alexander realized it was more than true. Lady Gertrude was every bit as skilled as the famous musicians he had intended to feature. It was astonishing.

"She's not showing off," Miss Finch said. "She's *hiding*, the inconsiderate scamp."

"Hiding?" Alexander repeated. "On stage in a ballroom?"

"Gertie disappears into her music every chance she gets. She could have been a celebrated pianist if she hadn't been born a lady, or if her father were less of a—" Miss Finch cleared her throat. "That is to say, Lady Gertrude is accomplished in all things. She could manage a dukedom just as well as she makes music."

"Subtle," he murmured.

"Is there any reason to be?" Miss Finch lifted a shoulder unapologetically. "Everyone under this roof knows this year's party is less Christmastide and more a Duchess Derby. My money is on Lady Gertrude."

He arched his brows. "I thought proper ladies didn't gamble."

"I'm not in the running," Miss Finch reminded him. "I'm as likely to dance atop a piano as play one. I would make a dreadful duchess. But I can help you find the right one."

He frowned. "I thought Lady Gertrude was the right one?"

"If you do think that, then my work here is over. But if you're still deciding, it is Gertie's wish that I help you make a sound choice. Just as she wouldn't wish to be trapped in an unhappy marriage, nor does she wish a poor match on you. I know the foibles and the families of every young lady in this room. I've watched them all for years. If you would like a lieutenant, I'm yours until Twelfth Night."

He stared at her. "This was Lady Gertrude's idea?"

"She insisted most vexingly."

Miss Finch did not look gratified.

"It's very... kind," he admitted. "Thoughtful and logical, indicative of a clever mind and the ability to think further than oneself and the present moment."

"Mm," said Miss Finch. "Almost as if she's perfect duchess material."

He narrowed his eyes. "You'd match me to someone other than your cousin?"

She pressed her lips together with obvious indecision and then sighed. "Like Gertie, I have no wish for either of you to be miserable for the rest of your lives. If what's best is for you to choose one of the other young ladies, then yes. I would help you make the most fitting match."

"Hm," said Alexander.

Almost as if Miss Finch was every bit as compassionate, logical, and forward-thinking.

He would not be surprised to discover Lady Gertrude had learned the traits by looking up to her cousin.

"Very well," he said. "I accept your assistance in this matter."

Miss Finch looked as though he had crushed her last dream.

"I figured you would," she said glumly. "It would've been so much easier if you'd simply fallen in love with Gertie at first sight."

"She's very pretty," he said automatically.

To be honest, all of the debutantes were pretty.

He supposed Miss Finch would say that was one of their necessary accomplishments. Their pastel gowns were flattering, their extravagant hair arrangements stunning, their movements in time to the country-dance rhythmic and graceful.

"I see what you mean." Miss Finch's gaze swung to the dance floor. "It must take mental fortitude not to fall in love with all of them at once."

Alexander's heart clenched.

It had not happened to her.

She'd looked just like this once, or whatever the equivalent had been twelve years ago. He couldn't recall the fabric colors and hair dressings of the day, but Alexander had no doubt Miss Finch would have copied them perfectly.

She was outrageous now, but back then, she'd been...

Unremarkable.

He couldn't recall a single thing about her from those days, despite the probability that they'd been at the same crushes dozens if not hundreds of times.

Then again, he hadn't been looking. Twelve years ago, he'd been an adolescent still adjusting to the role of duke, and the last thing he'd needed was to complicate his life with a bride.

And now here he was, presiding over a Duchess Derby in a ballroom awash with exceptional choices... spending his limited time at the side of a woman who would not do at all.

She wasn't in the running.

Miss Finch was his lieutenant.

Of course it was fine for a general to discuss strategy with his lieutenant.

Her gown was a bold purple, her blond tresses twisted into a careless bun rather than bedecked with curls.

He supposed saving time with one's toilette was one of the advantages of being a spinster.

The bold colors and unfussy hair suited her. The tiny laugh lines at the corners of her sparkling blue eyes did not remind him of her age, but rather evoked her infectious laugh and boisterous spirit.

Miss Finch probably *would* dance on a piano.

She probably *had* danced on a piano.

Alexander could not help but think he'd perhaps attended all of the wrong parties.

"Tell me," she said. "Which woman has caught your interest?"

"Er..." he replied eloquently.

Miss Finch raised her eyebrows as if she'd wait patiently all night for Alexander to help her help *him*.

"You said Lady Gertrude is hiding?" There. Her cousin was a perfectly safe topic. "What is she hiding from?"

"You," she answered without hesitation. "Gertie's shy. She's terrified of you."

"Me?" he sputtered. "I'm not frightening."

"Go and prove it to her." Miss Finch smiled innocently. "I promise any given debutante in this room will be delighted to show off her skill at the pianoforte, if you'd like to take this opportunity to invite Gertie to be your first dance partner of the Yuletide."

Diabolical logic.

"Very well played," he said with admiration. "I thought you were supposed to be *my* lieutenant, not Lady Gertrude's."

"How can you determine which young woman

is the right one, if you don't come to know them all?" Miss Finch pointed out. "You might as well begin with Gertie as anyone. I'll even spread a rumor that you'd like to see how the others stack up at the pianoforte."

"*Wait,*" he said, but of course Miss Finch did not.

By the time Lady Gertrude played the final notes of the country-dance, a queue had already started to form behind the bench with other young ladies eager to display their talent with music.

Alexander arrived at the dais just as the next melody began.

"What lucky happenstance," said Miss Finch. "It's a waltz."

"You *told* her to play a waltz," said Lady Gertrude.

Miss Finch shoved her into Alexander's arms. "Can't talk. Must join the other spinsters in the shadows. Have a lovely dance, you two."

She vanished into the crowd.

There was nothing left to do but waltz.

"Your cousin is terrifying," he told Lady Gertrude.

She brightened. "Cynthia Louise will be delighted to hear that. She always says, if you can't please someone, scare the pants off of them instead."

"That's something she *always* says?" he repeated, then replayed her words in his mind. "She thinks she doesn't please me?"

"She knows she doesn't please you," Lady Gertrude said. "If she pleased you, you would have married her years ago, before she was a spinster. Cynthia Louise says she doubts you even remember her at her come-out. She says the only reason you invite her to your Christmas parties is because your sister makes you."

All of that was... uncomfortably true.

"Belle can't 'make' me do anything," he said instead. "I'm a duke, and she's—"

"Not a spinster any longer." Lady Gertrude's eyes shone. "I just heard the news. How lucky to have found a love match!"

If only the rest of the beau monde would view it the same way.

"My sister wasn't a spinster," Alexander protested. "She was a... late bloomer."

"Then Cynthia Louise isn't a spinster either," Lady Gertrude said in satisfaction. "She's a flower, just like Belle."

Very neatly done. He couldn't argue without undermining his own assertion.

"Whose lieutenant are you?" he asked suspiciously.

"Cynthia Louise's." Lady Gertrude lowered her voice. "Don't tell her. She doesn't know."

"Why does she need one?" he asked. "She seems quite capable."

Lady Gertrude's eyes were almost pitying. "Everyone *needs* someone. The people who think they don't are the ones who need someone the most."

"Aren't you supposed to be shy?" he muttered.

"I usually am," she agreed, "but you asked me about Cynthia Louise, who is my favorite person in the world. I can't wait to tell her you think she's a flower."

"I didn't say that," he said quickly. "Don't tell her."

Miss Finch had orchestrated this waltz for Alexander to come to know her cousin, and instead he'd turned the topic to Miss Finch.

"Tell me about you," he said to Lady Gertrude.

Her expression shuttered and she stared over his shoulder without speaking.

"Your cousin wants us to talk," he reminded her. "About *you*."

She dragged her gaze back to his and visibly sucked in a restorative breath.

"Five feet tall, eight stone, youngest of three daughters to Lord and Lady Eddlestone, fluent in French, middling at mathematics, well versed in the running of a household, skilled at the pianoforte, reasonably talented with a needle, shockingly bad at watercolor, excellent at memorizing timetables and lists, and unapologetically partial to tragic operas with sad tenor solos."

He blinked. "It sounds like you memorized a spy's intelligence report... on yourself."

She nodded. "Cynthia Louise's idea. She said if I ever didn't know what to say, I could always use one of those things. Since this is an interview, I decided to use them all at once."

"It's not an interview," he said. "It's a waltz."

"It's an interview whilst waltzing," she amended. "How efficient of you! It must help with the hunt. You can quiz our brains while inspecting our looks up close and making certain we shan't embarrass you on the dance floor."

"That's not what I..."

Very well, fair enough.

Though such cold-bloodedness did not paint Alexander in the most favorable light.

"It's like any given Wednesday at Almack's," he tried to explain. "But smaller."

She nodded. "I appreciate that. It's much more relaxing. We've only to be terrified of you, rather than of a hundred gentlemen and half a dozen patronesses."

He glimpsed Miss Finch out of the corner of his eye. It was impossible to imagine her terrified of anything.

She was not dancing. That would have limited her to one swain. Instead, she held court between the biscuit table and the mulled wine. She was surrounded by a dozen locals who hung onto her every word, all of them snort-laughing together at some jest that involved comical facial expressions and wild gestures.

It was not at all the manner in which a lady was supposed to comport herself.

Yet there was no denying her allure.

The debutantes under this roof might have come here in hopes of a dukedom, but the local gentlemen were in this ballroom to be near the effervescent Miss Finch.

"Do you want to dance with her?" Lady Gertrude asked.

"Not at all," Alexander fibbed.

He could not dance with her. To do so would spark gossip, which was something he assiduously avoided. Alexander had spent his life striving to live up to societal expectations. Miss

Finch didn't bother pretending for a single moment.

Dancing with her was completely out of the question.

Completely.

"This year, I'll only dance with young ladies I'm considering as potential brides," he explained.

"Did you dance with her last year?" Lady Gertrude asked. "Or ever?"

No, he had not.

Even when not actively pursuing a bride, Alexander was mindful of his reputation. Cynthia playing at "lieutenant" for a fortnight skirted respectability closely enough.

He was not the sort of gentleman who told loud jests with big gestures and comical expressions, or snort-laughed with pretty spinsters next to the refreshment table.

But he suspected Lady Gertrude knew all of that.

She was remarkably astute.

"How old are you?" he grumbled.

"Eighteen years, one month, three days," she answered. "I'll add 'exact age' to the list for the next time I'm interviewed by a bride-hunting bachelor."

"If I choose you, there won't be a next time," he pointed out.

"It's still a good list. Cynthia Louise has one for everyone at the party."

He blinked. "She does?"

"Cynthia Louise knows everything," Lady Gertrude said. "She's the one who taught me to create mental lists. She says it helps with counting cards when gambling."

"Counting cards," Alexander said faintly. "When gambling."

"We practiced *vingt-et-un* during the carriage journey." Lady Gertrude frowned. "I'm dreadful at gambling. I should add that to the list."

"Don't add it to the list," he said quickly. "Leave some mystery."

Her eyes widened. "I hadn't thought of that. You're just as clever as Cynthia Louise."

Two days ago, Alexander might have believed that to be true. "She says she'll help me select my perfect match before the Twelfth Night ball."

"Of course she did." Lady Gertrude beamed at him. "That's what she said she was going to do."

"Are her claims always true?"

Lady Gertrude nodded. "But never how you think. If she says, 'Shall we go out for ices?'" it won't be Gunter's. She probably means to hike a fjord with a knapsack full of lemons in order to grate the virgin ice herself and make her own batch of lemon ice whilst sliding down a snow-covered mountain on skis."

The idea was preposterous.

Alexander could absolutely imagine Miss Finch doing it.

It was probably the story she'd been telling the locals over by his biscuit table.

"You do realize," he said, "the effect having her as a cousin has on your reputation."

Lady Gertrude nodded. "Everyone wishes they were me. Or Cynthia Louise."

Alexander blinked. As far as a not-so-veiled re-proof went, his rebuke had failed spectacularly.

"No," he said. "The young ladies are here be-cause they want to be a *duchess*."

"Or," said Lady Gertrude. "They want to be a duchess because they can't be Cynthia Louise."

The music stopped.

"Thank you for the waltz." She dipped an ex-quisite curtsey. "I'm going to drink three glasses of wine and spend the rest of the night playing ball with my puppy."

She was gone before Alexander could fathom a reply.

His sister Belle intercepted him on the edge of the dance floor. "Are you bored with your plan yet?"

"Not even a little bit," he said. "I'm not even certain what just happened."

He watched Miss Finch welcome her cousin into her circle with obvious delight and affection.

"Is that the one you're after?" Belle asked.

Alexander cut his gaze to her in horror. "A duke would *never*."

"I think Lady Gertrude is perfectly nice," Belle said. "Even Mother likes her."

Lady Gertrude.

Right.

"Did you know she weighs eight stone and is middling at mathematics?" he enquired.

"Eight stone," Belle murmured. "She should eat more biscuits."

"She also adores tragic operas."

"You hate tragic operas," his sister replied. "And now you've made one. You should call the whole thing off, Vale. This Christmastide bride hunt is a farce."

"A Duchess Derby, according to Miss Finch," he muttered.

"She's not wrong." Belle placed a hand on her chest. "What if... No, hear me out. *What if*... you looked for love instead of societal perfection?"

"There's no more foolish way to make a decision as important as marriage than to base it on one's heart," he snapped, then wished he hadn't. "No offense meant."

"All offense taken," she assured him. "You're disinvited to the wedding."

"Then who will give you away?"

"Very well, you can attend. But I will be miffed at you the entire time for having suggested love is foolish."

"Not for you," he allowed. "You're not a duke. I am."

And now he had to make an even better match to counteract her choice.

The perceived quality of his bride would affect the entire family—Belle, whether she liked it or not, their mother, the next generation of children... He did not take such heavy responsibility lightly.

"But a duke is not *all* you are, is it?" Belle patted his shoulder a bit too hard to be accidental. "What if you let these ladies come to know you? You've assembled the finest collection of duchessy debutantes in the country. Why not let love whittle it down from here?"

"Nobody needs to know me," he said. "The fact

that they're here means they've already decided in my favor."

"Nobody *does* know you," Belle corrected. "You don't let them. All they have to go on is Debrett's Peerage and the unending references in gossip columns to a certain handsome, wealthy Duke of N— who remains stubbornly single."

"What else is there to know?" he asked. "My voting record in the House of Lords? Whether I have any skill at embroidery or watercolor?"

"You've no skill at watercolor," his sister replied softly, "or any idea what it would feel like to have someone choose you for *you*." This time, her touch to his arm was gentle. "I wish you knew what you were missing."

"I'm not missing anything," he assured her. "I even have a lieutenant."

CHAPTER 5

*C*hristmas Day was an enormous celebration, second only to the grand Twelfth Night farewell ball the eve before Epiphany, upon which guests would return home carrying the news that the Duke of Nottingvale was betrothed to a future duchess.

Shortly after the sideboard was laid for breakfast, Alexander's halls were positively brimming with merrymakers and well-wishers.

Each Christmas, his house was open to everyone in the village—and everyone in the village took him up on the offer.

All of the parlors and drawing rooms were stocked with food and drink. He had not planned specific activities this afternoon due to the sheer number of people flowing in and out of the house. Villagers came to mingle with aristocracy. Party guests might slip away to attend church in the castle...

Or, in the case of his business partner Jonathan, sneak off to win the heart of the local jeweler.

It was lovely that some people could afford to let their hearts decide marital matters, truly it was, but Alexander had neither the time nor the freedom for nonsense.

Which was the only reason why he and Miss Finch hadn't left each other's sides all day.

The *only* reason.

She was his lieutenant in the battle to win a duchessy bride, and so far the operation was unfolding flawlessly.

"—in the cerulean dress," Miss Finch was murmuring into his ear. "She's nineteen, so not properly a debutante, but her first Season was superlative by any standard. She turned down no less than five proposals. Two from minor peers, one from an eye-wateringly wealthy textiles heir, and the others from heart-wrenchingly lovesick swains. Like you, she is not motivated by love or money, but rather—"

Miss Finch was the perfect height for murmuring into Alexander's ear. He could not help but admire this trait every time she did so. Modern fashions might consider her appallingly tall for a lady. But for a lieutenant, her height was absolutely perfect.

He was especially glad her blond tresses had been carelessly twisted into another plain, unadorned bun high above her nape.

If Miss Finch had taken the time to curl a few face-framing ringlets, as a lady ought, those soft tendrils might tickle against Alexander's shoulder every time she murmured into his ear, thus distracting him from the surprisingly detailed intelligence she had amassed on everyone she had ever met.

He was definitely not distracted.

He was paying very close attention.

To... what was she saying? Daughter of a marquess, cousin to the Speaker of the House of Commons, mm-hm, intriguing.

What was that light scent he caught whenever Miss Finch inclined ever so slightly in his direction? Was it a perfume? A soap? It was not-quite-flowery, which shouldn't surprise him in the least.

If Miss Finch went on a botany expedition for *eau de toilette*, she'd likely return with stinging nettles, a Venus Flytrap, and a stack of sticky honeycomb she'd nicked from beehives with her bare hands.

That was how she smelled. Chaotic and sweet and dangerous.

"—if she hadn't selected the wrong spoon in front of one of the patronesses of Almack's," Miss Finch concluded, apparently no longer singing the praises of the young lady in blue, but rather recounting the worst known scandal of an otherwise unobjectionable young lady in green.

"You seem to know Society's rules to the letter," he murmured to Miss Finch.

See? Another reason to be glad she hadn't curled ringlets into her hair. One soft tendril might have brushed against his mouth as he bent his head to hers, causing his mind to deviate from finding his future bride. Miss Finch's plainness had a purpose. It was *practical*. She was helping him to concentrate on his aims. Just as she'd promised to do.

"Of course I know society's rules." Her low, earthy chuckle tickled his skin beneath his clothes. "How else would I know how to break them?"

Was it too hot in here? Too cold? The fireplace was crackling, the windows ajar to allow in fresh air—surely that was the explanation for this strange sensation of not knowing how to feel in his own skin.

He wasn't *attracted* to her.

Here, he would prove how much they did not suit.

"Is it true you ran through the cascade fountains of Chatsworth House during a garden party?"

"I didn't *run*. I luxuriated in them."

She burst out laughing at his flinch of shock.

"In my defense," she said, "it was a hot day. We had been playing Pall Mall on the lawn. I'd tried to balance a lemonade whilst taking a swing at my ball, and ended up splashing half of it down my bodice. Changing clothes would've taken an hour, and we were *winning*. I was the only person in my group who knew what to do with a mallet, and my team depended on me. Whilst the others took their turn, I nipped over to the fountain to wipe the stickiness from my bosom as best I could. I might've been soaking wet, but I won the game."

See? Not an attractive picture *at all*.

He was definitely not imagining her hair clinging to her face in damp tendrils as she dabbed a wet handkerchief to her water-misted bodice.

So glad he'd asked for clarification on the idle gossip.

Brilliant move. Now that he had the true mental image to picture, he'd... he'd...

Never sleep soundly again from dreams of Miss Finch glistening with water like a siren from the sea as she swung her mallet to victory.

"Why are you invited anywhere?" he blurted out.

"Oh, I wasn't invited *back*," she said with a laugh. "But that was mostly due to the gentlemen being poor sports about losing a game of Pall Mall to a team of ladies. It seems men aren't as superior as they like to claim."

Or they were *distracted*.

By Miss Finch, who wasn't plain at all.

Which, Alexander supposed, only proved her point as to men's inferiority.

She was standing before him perfectly dry, and he still had no hope in heaven of hitting a ball in a straight line in his current state. All he could think about was holding the next party at his West Midlands manor, which had plenty of garden for installing cascading fountains.

"Ooh," she said. "I almost forgot about that one."

"What one?" he stammered. "What are we talking about?"

She touched his arm, either to hush him or to get his attention.

It hushed him and got his attention.

It was the briefest touch. Practically accidental. Just a brushing of knuckles against his forearm. A playful little nudge, as if *he* were the naughty imp, and she the stern matron tasked with keeping him in line.

Wonderful. Another fine image for his growing collection.

Miss Finch was singing the virtues of a different young lady. Alexander was paying close attention. Or would be, if he hadn't just now noticed that her extraordinary height wasn't only advantageous for murmuring into one another's ears, but also for kissing.

Not that he *would* kiss her.

He would never.

It was just that, for some other gentleman who happened to be as tall as Alexander, if he happened to be standing next to Miss Finch—their kiss would be a comfortable fit, was all. Just an observation. Nothing he intended to put into *practice*.

She sucked in a breath. "Damnable puppy! I'll return in a moment. Max appears to be sneaking cakes from plates left too low on side tables."

There.

Irrefutable proof—not that there had been any doubt—that Miss Finch was the opposite of acceptable.

Respectable ladies did not curse.

Respectable ladies did not bring their unleashed dogs to other people's parties uninvited and allow them to wreak havoc on the party's guests by stealing their tea cakes.

No matter how winsome the puppy was.

The cloying scent of his mother's perfume tickled Alexander's nose. "*Please* tell me you aren't entertaining the notion of Miss Cynthia Louise Finch."

Alexander clenched his jaw. He and his mother had already had one dreadful row, in which she railed that he'd "allowed" Belle to throw away her good blood at the expense of the family. If it were up to Mother, she'd put a stop to the union at once.

Luckily for Belle, who she wed was *not* up to their mother.

Unluckily for Alexander, *he* was now being scrutinized even closer than before. There was no room for error. Or for scandal.

"No," he said. "I am not courting Miss Finch. The idea is absurd. She and a dukedom are completely incompatible in every way."

He watched.

At this moment, she was cuddling a puppy and consoling her cousin, who appeared mortified to the point of apoplexy to discover a tea cake had been stolen.

And now Miss Finch was personally replacing the surrounding guests' repasts, presenting each with tiny plates piled high with cakes and biscuits.

And now she was saying something witty that involved so many expansive comical gestures that the poor puppy nearly tumbled off her bosom and into the closest tea cup.

And now the guests were howling with laughter, any earlier pique forgotten as they fought amongst themselves to be next in line to snuggle the adorable wiggly puppy.

"Ghastly behavior," said the Duchess of Nottingvale. "It's a wonder they didn't toss their tea into her face."

Alexander did not point out that the guests appeared merrier *after* Miss Finch's intervention than they had before it.

Or his suspicion that any tea dashed in her direction would soon be followed by a wet frolic through a public fountain.

"Don't worry," he said. "The primary requirement of any duchess is flawless comportment. I know my duty, and my duchess will perform hers."

"How goes the bride hunt?" his mother enquired. "Are you any closer?"

"It's been two days," he reminded her. "I have until Twelfth Night."

"Do you need twelve days? Belle assures me all of the debutantes present are so respectable, you could select the next one to walk by and not go astray. Then again, I cannot put stock in *her* judgment anymore."

He tensed. "She's happy, Mother. That's all that matters."

"To her, perhaps." The duchess sniffed.

Alexander was not used to being the Good One in the family. He and his sister had always both been Good Ones.

Belle had followed the rules just as carefully as he had.

Almost as carefully.

Very well, it appeared that what his sister had carefully accomplished was to hide her rule-breaking from others.

He'd always known Belle was a gifted artist, but he had *not* known she'd taken a post as an advertisement illustrator under a male pseudonym.

Mother still did not know.

Belle wasn't drawing announcements for Kew Gardens anymore. She was now the artist responsible for painting the fashion plates that would become aquatints in Alexander's new venture. "Fit for a Duke" was a collection of men's apparel, to be sold via catalogue.

He was not involved in any aspect of the trade, of course. He was the titular duke, and the primary investor. He provided a lump sum and would later reap the reward of interest returned, as was proper.

Belle had betrothed herself with the tailor.

This was... not proper, and the reason their mother was more fearful than ever that Alexander might make an inappropriate match. Any misstep could ruin the family beyond repair.

It wasn't as if Belle's "flagrant disregard" for the unblemished reputations of her family was *contagious*, for heaven's sake.

Alexander knew the rules. Unlike Miss Finch, he did not break them.

He made them into a game.

As a young boy, rule-following had been stifling, boring business. So he'd assigned points to each Do and Do Not, commensurate with his desire to do the opposite. The more he longed to bend a rule, the more points he earned for following it.

His running score was in the millions.

Mother's eyes flashed up at him. "You must choose wisely, Vale."

"I know." He let out a slow sigh. "*I know.*"

Happiness had naught to do with the matter.

He must content himself with "winning" the game. The satisfaction of having successfully followed the rules, exceeded his mother's high expectations, and made a decision that would reflect favorably on the dukedom for generations to come.

His family—existing *and* future—depended on him.

"You're a good man, Vale," his mother said. "If your father could see you now..."

He nodded stiffly.

Father had taught his only son to follow in his footsteps from the moment Alexander could toddle. Expectations for a future duke had been drilled into him from birth.

Alexander was raised in his father's image because that was how his own father had been raised. He came from a long line of exemplary dukes, and was expected to continue the tradition with his own heirs.

It was his duty.

For all thirty of Alexander's years, he strove to live up to his father's example. To be the sort of duke that would have made his father proud.

He would not stop now.

He would *never* stop doing everything in his power to be the best man, duke, and future husband and father he could be.

One day, his children would be emulating *him*.

As well as their mother.

"I'll choose a duchess by Twelfth Night," he promised his mother. "Someone worthy of the title."

She gave a sharp nod. "See that you do."

The moment she strode away, Alexander's sister Belle sneaked up from behind and grabbed hold of his arm.

"You know why Mother marched over here,

don't you? She saw you whispering with Cynthia Louise. Excellent work flying right past me in the 'unacceptable match' race." Belle cackled. "I love it. Cynthia Louise is everything I never dreamt you'd choose."

"I *didn't* choose her," he said stiffly. "She's helping me choose *someone else*."

"Mm-hm," said Belle. "Mayhap *Mother* believes that."

"I cannot make impulsive choices," he told her in exasperation. "The dukedom is on *my* shoulders. I cannot besmirch—"

"If this is about Father," Belle interrupted, "he'd be proud of you because you're a decent person, not because you wear the right fashions."

"It's not the clothes," Alexander said. "It's what's inside of them. *Me*. Father isn't here anymore… but you are. Mother is. My future heirs will be. I have to think about them."

"Can you think about making them with a wife you *like*?"

Alexander *hadn't* thought about that, to be honest.

His personal preferences had never entered into the decision-making process.

Perhaps there *was* a middle ground.

He would choose someone respectable and proper, as his mother and forefathers expected.

And he would try to make certain that person was someone he liked.

Surely it was possible.

He enjoyed his conversations with Miss Finch, and she wouldn't do at all. Conversations with the *right* person could only be better.

"Here she comes," Belle whispered. "Lure her in."

Alexander scowled at his sister, but she was already retreating into the crowd and therefore missed his irritated expression entirely.

A duke didn't need to *lure* anyone. One mention of Alexander's intent to take a bride, and the walls fairly shook from the effort of containing the plethora of contenders.

Not that Miss Finch was interested in being a contender, he was forced to admit.

If he wanted her to be—which he did not—his sister was probably right.

He'd have to lure her in.

"I'm going to lock Max in my bedchamber." Miss Finch motioned in the general direction. "Walk with me?"

Of course not.

That would be highly improper.

"I'll accompany you as far as the corridor," he said.

A dreadful idea, but no harm would come of it.

This was his house. He could stroll any corridor he pleased.

She was a *spinster*. A *chaperone*. She was here to keep nubile nymphs out of his arms, not to tempt his self-control herself.

There was absolutely no danger of anything untoward occurring.

Nothing at all.

"Your party is an unequivocal success," she said the moment the roar of the crowd was behind them. "But are *you* having any fun?"

"Dukes don't have fun," he explained to her. "Dukes have duty."

She made a face. "If *I* were a duke, I'd have nothing *but* fun."

"That's why there's a patriarchy," he muttered. "*Someone* has to manage things."

"I manage to have *fun*," she said with an unrepentant grin. "I brought skis. Do you want to try them?"

"I can't leave the party." He stared at her. "It's *my party*."

"Pah. I sneak out of parties like this all of the time. There are too many planned activities for anyone to notice. One summer, on a tour of Lord —" She broke off, her eyes widening. "Are you saying you *would* play at skis with me... if it weren't your party?"

"No skis," he said firmly. "No risking my life until there's an heir, and even then it's an irresponsible idea."

"Irresponsible but fun," she said. "You keep missing the point."

"Not everything is fun. What if I broke my leg?"

"I broke mine twice." Her eyes took on a far-off sparkle. "Eventually, I flew over that crevice."

"You jumped across a wide crevice?" he said in horror. "On skis?"

She nodded. "Fell *into*, twice. Soared *across*, once. Indubitably worth it. I won an astronomical wager."

"You're a madwoman," he informed her.

Part of him wished he'd been there to see her win the bet.

"One moment..." She and Max slipped into her guest chamber.

She closed the door behind them.

He tensed.

From the corridor, all Alexander could hear was what sounded like his very expensive furniture scraping across his equally expensive floors, followed by excited yips from the puppy, and a peal of laughter from Miss Finch.

She was out of breath and disheveled when she slipped back out of the door and closed it tight behind her.

"There," she said, the word husky and breathless. "What now?"

Now, Alexander was going to shove his hands behind his back and perform any magic necessary to keep himself from kissing her.

She grinned at him. "Cat got your tongue?"

There were many, many things Alexander would like to do with his tongue, none of which were appropriate thoughts toward Miss Finch.

He turned from her, heroically, all of the game-points in the world raining down around him in celebration of his stoic ducal restraint.

"I'm teasing," she said, and nudged at his arm the way she liked to do when she was poking verbally at him.

It might have resulted in nothing more than that, except Alexander had chosen that exact moment to start walking away from her. His stride bent his arm at such an angle that instead of nudging him with her knuckles, her fingers tangled with his.

They were now holding hands.

In the middle of his guest corridor.

"Er," Alexander said.

He should have let go of her hand by now.

He was going to.

Any second.

Miss Finch looked just as discombobulated. She had frozen still, which was the opposite of her natural state of human hurricane. Color rose up her cheeks.

They were very nice cheeks. They led the eye to her plump, kissable lips.

Which had parted, either in anticipation of the kiss that hung in the air between them, or because she too struggled for air.

He dropped her hand.

"My apologies," he said gruffly.

She touched her fingers to her mouth, and then to her chest. "None needed."

"I should not have touched you." Why was he going on about this?

She nodded. "I should not have let you."

"Then we understand each other," he said.

He understood very, very well.

Under no circumstances could they be alone together again.

Especially if it might lead to *fun*.

CHAPTER 6

*C*ynthia Louise stared down at the straw she'd drawn.

After spending last night and all morning keeping every subsequent interaction with Nottingvale as formal and lieutenant-ish as possible, of *course* they'd been randomly assigned to the same team for the evening game of charades.

Each group of performers was spread out in pockets throughout the ballroom, leaving the raised wooden dais open for the pantomimes.

Cynthia's team consisted of the Duke of Nottingvale, three debutantes, said debutantes' mothers and chaperones—who had *not* been assigned to the group, but hovered over their charges' shoulders protectively—as well as the duke's tailor and future brother-in-law, Mr. McAlistair.

Gertie's group consisted of both local blacksmiths, the local dairy farmer, the local baker, the castle solicitor, and Lady Isabelle, the duke's sister. Gertie's group was on the opposite side of the ballroom.

It was going to be impossible to matchmake from here.

"I could switch places with Lady Gertrude," Cynthia said.

"You can't switch places," snapped one of the mothers, who hadn't been assigned to this group at all. "Straws were drawn for a reason."

"I'm surprised you're here at all," said one of the other mothers. "I thought I saw you *leaving the party* after breakfast."

"*Uncivilized*," sniffed another.

"I had to leave after breakfast," Cynthia said. "Don't you read the Cressmouth Gazette? Today was the final ice carving demonstration in the castle park."

"You were gone for *hours*. How long can it take to look at ice sculptures?"

"I've no idea," Cynthia said with a shrug. "I can tell you it took two hours and thirty-six minutes to attempt to carve a completely unrecognizable frozen facsimile of a partridge."

"You were *in* the ice-carving competition?" Nottingvale closed his eyes. "Of course you were."

"I finished in last place," she said cheerfully. "It was glorious. Let me know if you'd like to decorate your garden with frozen blobs that in no way resemble bird-like creatures."

"Lady Gertrude is such a treasure," whispered one of the mothers. "How can she be related to... *her?*"

"Gossip is far more gauche than ice-sculpting," Cynthia informed her haughtily. "Although I suppose at least you didn't wait to do it behind my back."

"She also does it behind your back," the daughter whispered.

"I know," Cynthia whispered back.

Twelve years ago, when bright-eyed Cynthia Louise Finch was a brand-new debutante, the gossip had crushed her soul. She was a lump of clay. No, not a lump of clay—clay could be molded into something serviceable. She was just a lump. No one with any brains would wander into a patch of wallflowers with *her* in it, they said.

Six years of that balderdash later, she'd had enough. If she was to be gossiped sorrowfully about for achieving nothing, then she might as well be gossiped about for achieving *something*.

Her circle of friends increased exponentially. Oh, there were no more vouchers to Almack's and the like, but those stultifying evenings were replaced by poetry readings and battledore tournaments and political debates and learning how to fence.

It was leagues better than being a wallflower. And, if these matrons were paragons of their class, apparently better than being wife to a lord, as well.

Who cared if no one had ever asked Cynthia for her hand? She was too busy for a husband. She could barely squeeze in an hour or two of matchmaking between all of the ice carving and sled races. She might have once dreamt of love, but enjoying life on her own terms was much better than failing to live up to someone else's.

"So," murmured the Duke of Nottingvale. "Not these girls?"

"The young ladies themselves are perfectly charming," she murmured back. "It's their mothers who have forgotten their manners. Just watch the performance."

Indeed, the other teams were darling at charades, many of them quite talented.

Soon enough, all eyes turned to their corner.

"It's *our* turn?" gasped one of Cynthia's teammates, as if they were all to be shot by firing squad.

Another clutched a scrap of foolscap with their assigned subject printed inside.

Cynthia plucked the trembling paper from her hand. "It says 'Mail Coach.' That's simple enough. Go on, then. Nottingvale, you can be the driver—"

"*Me?*"

"Then you two can be horses, which leaves the others to be passengers and... *you* to try and purchase a ticket to ride on top." She handed the paper back.

"On top?" the debutante squeaked. "I would never travel by mail coach."

"It's one of life's greatest pleasures," Cynthia informed her. "And also this is charades. Your friends have never been horses. You're to *pantomime.*"

She shooed them all toward the dais, whilst staying behind with the mothers and chaperones to watch.

"I wish it was my Hortense deciding amongst a sea of suitors," said one of the mothers wistfully.

Cynthia couldn't fathom hosting an entire soirée of aristocratic suitors. She imagined deciding between dozens of men would cause just as much anxiety as not having any interest at all.

As much as she loved Gertie, playing duenna to

a pretty young marriageable thing was an exercise in walking around with constant evidence of one's unsuitability.

She pressed her lips together.

At thirty years old, Nottingvale could barely fit all of the eager young ladies under one roof.

At thirty years old, Cynthia Louise Finch was considered a dusty, dried-up relic.

In that sense, the mothers were right to caution their daughters not to end up like her. For women who wished to marry well, there was a short window of desirability.

Debutantes were like young tomatoes. A little green, a little unripe, and in danger of being sent back to the scullery the moment blemishes appeared.

"They guessed it!" the young ladies crowed as they skipped back to the group. "We're to go one more time."

"You do it." One of the pink-cheeked debutantes shoved a paper into Cynthia's hand. "After playing a horse, I cannot show my face again."

Cynthia unfolded the paper.

"'Romeo and Juliet.'" She cast a dry look toward Nottingvale. "Forbidden love. Who could possibly believe that your family would disapprove of you making a match with me?"

"It practically writes itself," he murmured. "Shall we attempt the balcony scene?"

But soft! What light through yonder window breaks? It is the east, and Juliet is the sun. Arise, fair sun, and kill the envious moon...

Cynthia shook the wistful image from her

head. "Too romantic. It'll confuse everyone. Let's skip to the poison and the stabbings."

She took her place on one side of the dais and motioned him to the other.

As dramatically as possible, she pantomimed unstoppering a bottle and drinking the poison within, making certain to stagger drunkenly for a few steps before crumpling to the floor like a corpse.

Only then did she remember how Romeo died.

He entered Juliet's tomb and kissed her lips before consuming the poison himself.

After which, Juliet awoke, and kissed *Romeo's* lips, before resorting to the dagger.

Her heart clattered.

In this version, there would be no kissing.

Would there?

No, definitely not. She just had to lie there with her eyes shut, corpse-like, whilst Nottingvale pretended to break into her tomb and become overset at the sight of her death, causing him to swallow what remained of the poison.

She held her breath.

Was he in her invisible tomb?

Had he drunk the poison yet?

The trouble with charades was the lack of dialogue to let one follow along with one's lover's path to self-destruction.

There was no way to know if it was time to wake up unless she peeked.

Cynthia cracked open one eye.

Nottingvale's face was inches from hers.

A tiny, un-corpse-like gasp escaped from between her parted lips.

He wasn't *really* going to kiss her... was he?

If he did, she would have to play her role, and kiss him back when it was her turn. Here, on the dais. In front of three dozen hopeful debutantes and their gimlet-eyed chaperones.

She hoped he would.

She prayed he wouldn't.

His face retreated from hers, and her heart lurched in... Relief? Sorrow?

She squeezed her eyes shut.

He lifted her hand, which was not in the script at all.

He drew her fingers to his lips, which was *definitely* not in the script.

He pressed her palm to his chest, beneath which, his heart beat as erratically as her own. Her entire body seemed to pulse in syncopation with his. Wanting. Waiting. Wondering.

She couldn't look.

She daren't look.

Her hand was placed gently back on her midsection, followed by a poignant pause in which Nottingvale was presumably consuming the last of her poison.

An ungainly thump shook the dais as he fell lifeless to the wooden floor beside her.

The ballroom was unearthly silent.

Surely by *now*, someone should have guessed the play, making it completely unnecessary for Cynthia to "awaken" and pretend to kiss Nottingvale's lips.

Not a whisper sounded in the still chamber.

Very well.

Cynthia shot upright with a loud gasp.

Several of the debutantes squeaked in terror.

Cynthia cast wild-eyed glances about her "tomb" before noticing her lifeless Romeo lying still beside her.

With exaggerated expressions of panic and horror, she scooped up both of Nottingvale's hands and pressed the bare knuckles to her bosom —*take that, you scoundrel*—before bending down as though she intended to kiss his lips.

She didn't move.

No one moved.

Nottingvale's hands were still clutched to her breasts.

The duke cracked open one warm brown eye. He flinched to discover her face floating mere inches above his and immediately squeezed his eyes back shut.

He deserved it.

She cradled his fingers to her bosom for a moment longer before tossing his hands to his chest, drawing an imaginary dagger from his hip, and plunging the invisible blade into her gut for a slow, dramatic death, culminating in her lifeless body slumped against his side.

A beat of silence.

Another beat of silence.

Wild, one-person applause accompanied by a familiar squeal, and her cousin's cry of, "Brava, Cynthia Louise! Brava! Oh, and Nottingvale, you were fine, too!"

"Romeo and Juliet!" came the shout from all corners of the ballroom.

Cynthia opened her eyes and tilted her head on the wooden floor toward the duke.

He was watching her, a slight smile playing on his lips and an unreadable expression in his eyes.

She smiled back shyly.

Shy. *Her.*

Cynthia Louise Finch.

He leapt up and pulled her to her feet, keeping one hand clasped in his. He made an exaggerated bow. She dipped in a magnificent curtsey.

"I believe they won," someone called out. "That means it's time for wine and cakes!"

The clumps of straw-drawn teammates burst into motion like the explosion of white seeds from a late-summer dandelion.

"I should go," she told Nottingvale. "Who knows what Max has done to the guest room."

He dropped her hand but didn't step away. "I'll walk with you. In case I need to authorize the complete replacement of every stick of furniture in that chamber."

"Don't order until the end of the party," she suggested. "Then you'll only have to do it once."

As they exited the ballroom and entered the corridor, they ran into Nottingvale's business partner Mr. MacLean carrying a life-size, extremely well dressed, wicker doll.

"That thing is as big as you are!" Cynthia exclaimed.

"It ought to be," said Mr. MacLean. "It's modeled in Nottingvale's image."

"Why are you carrying it through my house?" asked the duke. "For a *second* time."

"Angelica told me to give it back," he explained, though it explained nothing.

"Why do you have a well-dressed wicker doll

modeled after your proportions?" Cynthia asked Nottingvale as his business partner disappeared around the corner.

"It's a new venture," he said hesitantly, as if uncertain what she'd make of it. "We're selling inexpensive men's apparel via catalogue, in order to offer high fashion to those who would not otherwise be able to afford it."

"That's... marvelous." She stared at him, feeling as though she were seeing him for the first time. "I don't know what I thought your explanation was going to be, but 'bringing men's fashion to the masses' was not on the list. I think your venture sounds lovely."

"I hope everyone else feels the same. We hope to begin next month. We've an entire stack of fashion plates, all illustrated by Mr. MacLean with aquatints designed by my sister Belle. The next step is arranging the printing. My man of business wrote this morning to say—" Nottingvale scrunched up his nose and glanced away. "I'm blathering on."

"I didn't know you *could* blather on" she admitted. "I find I like it."

Worse, she found she liked *him* even more than she had feared.

As if it weren't enough to merely be titled and filthy rich and mind-bogglingly handsome, Nottingvale had to also be a good sport and compassionate and friendly.

It was unfair.

Cynthia admiring his pretty trappings was bad enough, but developing a soft spot for the man he was inside...

Unacceptable comportment.

She increased her pace, reaching her closed bedchamber door in less than a dozen brisk strides.

"Thank you for seeing me safe to my door," she said. "Goodbye."

He didn't leave.

She didn't flee into the safety of her chamber.

Her heart beat faster.

"I should have kissed you," he murmured.

She stared up at him, which wasn't nearly far enough away. If she'd been of average height, she'd have an exceptional view of his cravat at the moment. Instead, her eyes were level with his lips. Which were at a temptingly close kissing distance.

"I *would* have kissed you," he amended, "but I wasn't certain if our audience would recall the staging for that scene as written."

Oh, yes. By all means.

Faithless interpretation of Shakespeare's theatrical wishes was the major conflict they ought to be discussing.

"You shouldn't kiss me," she forced herself to say. "You should marry my cousin."

Even *she* wasn't convinced by the emptiness of her words.

Her make-believe poison bottle had more substance than Cynthia's desire not to kiss Nottingvale.

He was right.

He should definitely have kissed her whilst they'd had the chance.

And the excuse.

Her pulse fluttered. She pretended not to be affected.

"I'm not married yet," he said. "Or betrothed, or promised, or anything of the kind."

"Yes," she said. "That's the problem your guests have been summoned to solve."

But it wasn't what he was talking about at the moment, and she knew it.

His lips were *so close*.

He lowered his head slightly. "What if—"

Loud *yaps* sounded from the other side of the door.

"Max," she stammered. "He's going to scratch through your expensive door and maul me through my stockings."

Mayhap she shouldn't have mentioned her stockings.

"Ah." Nottingvale took a half-step back. "I would never put you in danger."

"I put myself in danger all of the time," she babbled. "Like the time I invited the bachelor host of a Christmastide party to follow me unaccompanied down an empty corridor because I secretly wished he would kiss me even though it's a dreadful idea from all angles and—why am I telling you this?"

His eyes darkened and he reached for her.

"Cynthia Louise!" came a sunny voice from down the hall. "I should've known you'd attend to Max. Shall I return to the ballroom?"

"*Gertie*. What wonderful timing! Do come save me from myself, if you wouldn't mind, darling." Cynthia fumbled for the door handle, scarcely registering the feel of Max's little paws climbing her legs. "Lovely chat, Nottingvale. I'm sure you're anxious to get back to your party. All those future duchesses under one roof."

"That was rude," Gertie said when Cynthia all but slammed the door in their host's handsome face.

"It wasn't rude," Cynthia told her. "It was self-preservation."

Gertie drew herself up straight, eyes flashing. "If that blackguard—"

"Not *him*, darling. *Me*. I'm supposed to be matchmaking him to *you*, not kissing him in the corridor."

Gertie squealed and clapped her hands. "You *kissed* him?"

"I did not," Cynthia said quickly, grateful it was true. "But... I wanted to."

"You should have," Gertie said. "We all thought he was going to up there on the stage."

"He was acting," Cynthia reminded her.

Gertie shrugged. "It didn't look like it."

"You're not listening to me." Cynthia scooped up the bouncing puppy and tried again. "I'm failing you. I'm supposed to be driving his attention in your direction, and instead he looks at me like... like..."

"Like he's not pretending when he says he wants to kiss you?"

"*Yes*," she burst out desperately. "Exactly like that! I am a horrid chaperone and an even worse matchmaker."

"But you're a wonderful cousin," Gertie said. "Only an idiot would fail to see your charms, and Nottingvale is clearly a clever man."

"You're not helping," Cynthia muttered.

"I'm not trying to help," Gertie said. "I don't want to marry Nottingvale. I never did. He scares me, but he doesn't scare you. I'd be a wretched match for him, and you know it."

Cynthia closed her eyes. She *did* know it. That didn't change the facts.

"If I return you home without a betrothal—"

"Who said without a betrothal?" Gertie took Max from Cynthia. "I said not a *duke*. I didn't say no one. The tavern-keeper's son—"

"—is the son of a tavern-keeper. Your father would send me to Newgate before he'd allow that union to happen."

"Then you'll find the right suitor." Gertie beamed at her with complete confidence. "You're a wonderful matchmaker, Cynthia Louise. You've matched yourself to the Duke of Nottingvale—"

"He wants to *kiss* me, not court me."

"—and if there's a gentleman out there for me, you'll find him." Gertie snuggled her face between Max's floppy ears. "I wish I didn't have to marry anyone at all, but I trust you." Her smile wobbled. "If you say you've found someone who will please Father *and* me, I promise not to say no."

"Oh, Gertie." Cynthia pulled her cousin and the puppy into her embrace. "I wish you didn't have to marry until you were ready either. I wish all of the debutantes at this party had time to be themselves before they're forced to become someone else."

But they didn't have time.

They had five days.

CHAPTER 7

*B*y the following evening, the ballroom had devolved into mutiny.

It was time to dance. The famous musicians from London had not arrived. Might never arrive.

As much as the debutantes wished to impress Nottingvale with how accomplished they were at the pianoforte, none of them wanted to miss their opportunity to dance with the duke.

"I'll do it," said Gertie. "I'll play for the rest of the party."

Cynthia swung out an arm to block her cousin's forward movement. "*No.* I shan't make you marry anyone who doesn't suit, including the duke, but there are dozens of other gentlemen in this ballroom. If you're not going to entertain the thought of Nottingvale, then you must promise every dance with a new gentleman until you find someone you like."

"*Every* dance?" Gertie repeated doubtfully. "What if I played the pianoforte for eight out of ten dances? I *like* the pianoforte. I would marry the pianoforte. The pianoforte and I are an excellent match."

"Tell that to your father," Cynthia said, then wished she hadn't.

Gertie *had* told her father. It had been the only occasion in Cynthia's knowledge of Gertie standing up for herself to the earl.

It had been a disaster.

A *"professional"* pianist? bellowed the earl, his face livid. *No daughter of mine...*

Gertie hadn't got a single word in edgewise.

Afterward, she rarely spoke at all. Not to her father. She poured her frustrations into the keys and disappeared into her music.

I'll turn that deuced contraption into kindling, said the earl. *If you haven't a suitor by the end of the year, I'll find one for you!*

Four days remained, and already the earl had made good on his promise. An oily lech who thought nothing of trading a choice piece of land for a bride forty years his junior.

Unless Cynthia worked a Christmas miracle before the end of the party.

"Promise me," she told Gertie. "You'll dance with a different man every set until you've met them all. And you'll *consider* them. You'll try to talk and be yourself and see if you might suit. After we find your match, I'll break the news of your betrothal to your father."

Gertie's face was white, but she nodded jerkily. "I'll dance."

"You have no choice," Cynthia said softly. "Not if you want any hope to control your future. Meanwhile—"

Meanwhile, the Duke of Nottingvale had just stepped into view.

Her breath caught.

Cynthia supposed she was meant to be awestruck by the whiteness of his cravat and the exquisite tailoring of his coal black breeches and tailcoat, but when she looked at him all she could think of was how it felt *not* to see him.

When she'd been lying on the dais with her eyes shut tight. Waiting for him to come to her. Wondering if he would kiss her. Cracking open one eye and discovering him...

There.

"I don't suppose you can summon a pianist," he said gruffly.

"Er," Cynthia said.

Gertie did a horrendous job of looking away from the pianoforte.

"I'll do it," Cynthia said before her cousin's resolve weakened.

Nottingvale looked startled. "You can play the pianoforte?"

"I can climb a tree and shoot a pistol."

"What has that to do with the pianoforte?"

Fair enough.

"I know a few tunes," she assured him. "And I'm all you've got."

He glanced over his shoulder at the encroaching army of debutantes eager for a dance, then swung his resigned gaze back to Cynthia. "All right, go. Play a melody we can dance to. Thank you."

And with that, he disappeared into the sea of adoring young ladies.

"You know what to do," said Gertie.

"*You* know what to do," countered Cynthia. "Find someone your father would deem at least somewhat acceptable. No falling in love with a footman."

Gertie brightened. "Like Horace and Morris?"

"Especially not a matched pair of strapping country footmen. Your father would expire on the spot."

"And then I could marry the footmen *and* be a professional pianist," Gertie said dreamily. "All at the same time."

Cynthia turned her cousin's shoulders around to point her toward a shamefully overlooked group of *ton* bucks and dandies. Gertie had met them all during her come-out. "Fish in that pond first."

Gertie took a deep breath and set off to stroll within eyesight of beau monde approved rakes and bucks.

Cynthia hurried to the pianoforte and placed her fingers above the keys.

She *did* know what to do.

Give Nottingvale something to dance to.

The rousing, bawdy opening bars to *A Soldier Goes A-Wenching* burst from the pianoforte as Cynthia's fingers flew merrily over the keys.

Rather, *A* Spinster *Goes A-Wenching*.

Nottingvale shot her a wide-eyed glance of abject horror.

She puckered her lips in the form of a kiss without breaking the flow of music and transitioned seamlessly into a traditional country dance.

Only Nottingvale and the naughtier of the gentlemen had recognized the ribald tune before the familiar melody of *Mr. Beveridge's Maggot* filled the ballroom.

Pairs were made and patterns formed as the company squared off into the dance.

Luckily for Nottingvale, Cynthia knew more than enough reels and quadrilles to keep the party dancing from now until Twelfth Night.

Unluckily for Cynthia, the raised dais was a perfect vantage point from which to watch Nottingvale dance with pretty young lady after pretty young lady after pretty young lady.

The debutantes were right.

This was a terrible view.

She tried to concentrate on the keys, rather than the duke whirling other women about the dance floor.

Cynthia didn't want or need to know what it might feel like to dance in the duke's arms in front of all and sundry. Proximity to Nottingvale addled her brain. Their hands had touched on no less than three separate occasions, and the memory still caused palpitations.

A proper dance would kill her.

And a kiss...

She *did* want one, damn him.

Even though he wasn't courting her, a kiss would allow her to live the fantasy, just for a moment.

And only a moment.

If the thought of being a duchess terrified Gertie, to Cynthia the prospect was positively laughable.

She could follow rules if she wanted to, but she *didn't* want to.

Cynthia didn't give a flying fig about fitting in with the world that had shunned her, year after year, no matter how slavishly she'd followed its arbitrary conventions.

She'd rather be single forever than wade back into that cesspool.

Even for a duke.

Gertie was the more pressing concern.

Cynthia didn't wish to alarm her cousin, but she would not be at all surprised to learn the earl had a marriage contract drafted and ready, in case Cynthia failed to match Gertie with the duke.

Her heart ached.

Cynthia was well past the age of majority, but for Gertie it was still years away. If they didn't find someone reasonably respectable to pair her off with, the earl would have her in front of the altar by January.

This would be Gertie's final fortnight of freedom before beginning an entire lifetime of misery.

Cynthia could not allow that to happen.

She wanted Gertie to be happy. If that meant marrying a tavern-keeper's son or a footman, Cynthia didn't care in the least.

The earl, on the other hand, would have no scruple breaking an unadvantageous contract in order to pack Gertie off to a roué willing to pay for the privilege of possessing her.

There had to be someone in this ballroom capable of mollifying the earl *and* being a good husband to Gertie.

Cynthia prayed Gertie found the lad quickly.

Three in the morning tolled by the time Cynthia played the final *boulanger*.

The crowd had dwindled down to the last dozen or two dancers. If the other guests were like Cynthia, they had their eyes on the morning balloon ascent advertised in the Cressmouth Gazette.

The revelers who remained were either slogging through the last steps or slumped tipsily against the wall between the decimated refreshment table and the door.

When she played the final chord, Nottingvale bid each of his guests a good night.

After the final straggler exited the ballroom, the duke climbed up the dais to the pianoforte and sat down on the wooden bench next to Cynthia.

"Thank you," he said softly. "You saved the evening."

She stretched her fingers. "What's a ditty or two between friends?"

"You played for five hours," he pointed out. "Without stopping."

She hadn't done so for him.

She'd done so for Gertie.

Oh, very well, Cynthia had helped for his sake, too.

"Interesting opening," he said.

She grinned at him. "I'd hoped you'd like it."

He gestured at the ivory keys. "I'm ready to hear your inappropriate alternate lyrics."

She folded her hands in her lap primly. "Guests are asleep, Your Grace. It would not do to wake them up to the sound of my skill with rhyming 'rocked me fore and aft' with 'the length of his shaf—'"

Nottingvale closed the lid of the pianoforte.

"You're right," he said hastily. "They're not prepared for the nuance of your lyrics."

She shook her head in resignation. "No one ever is."

Nottingvale cleared his throat. "Speaking of—"

"Turgid shafts?" she supplied hopefully.

"*Music*," he corrected firmly. "You were wonderful tonight. Really."

"I'm not embarrassing," she admitted. "But I'm also not Gertie."

"Your cousin was astonishing at the pianoforte the other day," he agreed.

"Every day, if Gertie can help it. If you think she has a knack with songs by Playford or Gallini, you should hear the arias and cotillions she's invented on her own."

His surprise was evident. "Lady Gertrude composes her own music?"

Cynthia nodded. "Scores of it. Literally."

He seemed to think this over. "Do you think she'd agree to—"

"*No.*"

Of course Gertie would agree to be the party's official pianist. She'd sleep on this bench every night just to be closer to a pianoforte.

"I'll do it," Cynthia said. "Gertie needs to dance. I'll play for the rest of the party, if you need. I wasn't going to dance anyway."

He frowned. "Why not?"

"I never stood up for a set, back when I was

hoping to dance," she reminded him. "No longer trying makes it less awkward for everyone."

He didn't look convinced.

"Besides, I have things to do," she said quickly.

"You can't do other things whilst entertaining at the pianoforte," he pointed out.

"That's just at night. During the day, I've *so* many activities planned, I'd need to double myself to have a prayer of seeing them all. Oh, not *here*," she assured him. "All of the fun things are happening out in the village."

"As the host of this party," he said, "I should be offended by such a statement."

"As a guest of this party," she replied, "I should be offended that it's true."

He glared at her.

She grinned at him.

"Come with me," she said impulsively.

To her surprise, he looked tempted. "I can't. I'm the host. I'm stuck here every second of every day."

"Do you always do what you're supposed to do?"

"Yes," he answered simply.

She patted his hand. "That's too bad."

"*Almost* always." He trapped her hand in his.

She stared at him.

He lifted her fingers to his lips. Slowly. Deliberately.

This time, he wasn't playacting at charades for an audience.

This time, his actions were for her.

"Are we reenacting the moment?" she asked. She meant her tone to be flippant, but instead it sounded eager and unsteady. "Should I smash your hands to my breasts next?"

"I am exceedingly amenable to that suggestion," he said. "But first..."

He lowered her palm to his heart and angled his head until his mouth hovered a mere breath above hers. "May I kiss you?"

"Be quick," she whispered. "I have things to do."

"No. You have *this*."

And he kissed her.

His lips were soft and firm, at first gentle, then more demanding.

He hadn't been stalling, she realized. He'd been containing himself. Wrapping himself tight in the should-dos because to cut the strings that tied his hands...

Would lead to moments like *this*.

This wasn't one kiss. It was ten.

A hundred kisses.

Her fingers were no longer splayed on his chest, but diving into his hair, clutching him to her. He showed no sign of letting go.

His hands cupped her face, cradling her gently even as he demanded entry into her mouth, claiming her with his tongue as well as his mouth.

This was a different kind of kiss.

Shockingly intimate and deliciously erotic.

She had goosebumps everywhere, despite being enveloped by his heat, with her bodice pressed tight against his chest.

A spinster could get used to kisses like these.

Cynthia could get used to Nottingvale, in specific.

Breathless, she broke the kiss while she still could.

Within a week he would be betrothed to some other woman. It would not do to indulge a tendre for a man she could not keep.

Cynthia was not so silly as to risk her heart.

She hoped.

CHAPTER 8

*A*lexander was spoilt for choice.

He had met all of his potential brides, spoken with all of his potential brides, dined with all of his potential brides, danced with all of his potential brides...

And he was no closer to betrothing himself with any of them.

The Yuletide party was performing its function splendidly. It was Alexander who was dragging his feet.

In order to allow his guests time to sleep, he had planned no morning activities other than breakfast, which was laid out on the dining room sideboard at dawn and kept fresh until luncheon.

Afternoon activities were many and varied, most of them arranged by his mother. Society rules dictated that a female hostess preside over house parties, and Alexander's mother was happy to fill that role until her son could produce a wife.

Alexander was happy, too. Those same rules kept his guests entertained and his mother busy, leaving him free to moon out of a side window unobserved.

Where had Miss Finch gone at eight o'clock in the morning?

Why had she been *awake* at eight o'clock in the morning?

Was she ever coming back to the party?

For years, it had been her habit to slip away for an hour or two, usually in the mornings before the day's engagements began.

But last night, she had been up late playing the pianoforte. And kissing Alexander. Who had barely slept as a consequence, except to dream of kissing her again.

Nuncheon had come and gone with no sign of Miss Finch.

Guests were playing Commerce in the blue drawing room, dicing in the red parlor, performing a pantomime in the ballroom, taking chocolate and chatting in the dining room...

Not Miss Finch.

She had *things* to do.

He wondered what they were. And if, whilst doing them, she occasionally recalled certain kisses she'd shared with the Duke of Nottingvale.

Whose Yuletide party she was *supposed* to be attending.

A knock on the front door sounded down the corridor.

Alexander strode to investigate. He arrived just as his butler Oswald opened the door to reveal Miss Olive Harper, heiress to and manager of the famous Harper stud farm at the entrance to Cressmouth.

"Happy Christmas, Olive," said Alexander.

"It's a dreadful Christmas," she replied. "I'm going to murder my father. My sworn enemy is here to court me and he didn't bring any attire suitable for the weather. Is your business partner here? Mayhap he'll let me borrow the clothes from his manikin. They seem about the right size."

"If it's for your sworn enemy," Alexander said politely, "why not let him suffer his own poor choices?"

Olive let out an aggrieved sigh. "It's complicated."

He understood complicated.

"I have entire wardrobes full of prototypes we've developed," he informed her. "I can send over a trunk in no time. How long is your enemy staying?"

"Too long," Olive answered. "Ten days."

"Does he need anything else?"

She bit her lip. "Riding boots. If you have them. And he's rather wide in the shoulders, with thick biceps and defined thigh muscles, if you could ask your tailor to adjust the seams. He's a large man. Large and... very well shaped."

Ah. So it *was* complicated.

"I'll have it sent over at once," he assured her.

"Thank you." She looked simultaneously relieved and panicked, as if she suspected this new development might cause her undoing.

Alexander could understand that, too.

She left before he could ask any further questions.

He knew where to find his business partner, Calvin. Alexander's yellow parlor had been converted into a makeshift workroom, due to its exceptional light. Tailoring projects were piled on every surface.

He sent a pair of footmen to collect the most wintery prototypes from the dressing room, then explained what Olive needed to Calvin.

"Large," Calvin repeated. "And very well shaped."

"I believe she mentioned wide shoulders... thick biceps and thigh muscles..."

"'Sworn enemy,' she said." Calvin glanced about at all of the fashions filling the room. "To be clad in the finest men's apparel ever designed."

"'Complicated,' she said," Alexander reminded him. "How long do you need?"

"To let out a few seams?" Calvin shrugged. "An hour or two."

"Thank you. Let me know when you're finished. I'll have a footman deliver the trunk."

At least, that *had* been the plan.

But two hours later, the clothes were hemmed, the trunk was packed, and there was still no sign of Miss Finch at the party. One shouldn't have anything to do with the other, but...

"I'll deliver the trunk," Alexander announced to his footmen, who looked appropriately aghast.

"I'll summon a coach," said the butler.

And Alexander would stare out of the carriage window looking for signs of Miss Finch.

He put on his hat and coat and was halfway to the door when his mother stepped around the corner.

"Vale," she said in obvious surprise. "Are you going somewhere?"

"I have to pay a quick call to the Harpers. Can you manage things here for the next twenty or thirty minutes?"

She looked amused. "I 'manage' them for the entire fortnight. That's why you must choose the perfect duchess. Your presence at parties is practically superfluous, because it is your hostess to whom all eyes will be constantly fixed. I am happy to take her under my wing, but she must have the appropriate potential."

"Yes, Mother," he said gently. "I'm aware of the qualifications for the perfect bride."

"Of course you are." She gave a sharp nod. "I won't keep you from your errand. Supper will be at half past eight. I've arranged the seating so that you are between two of the likeliest contenders, and right across from another."

"Thank you, Mother," he said. "You do think of everything."

She looked pleased at this, and continued down the corridor without another word.

Alexander dashed to the coach before anyone else could waylay him.

The Harper farm was on the outskirts of the village. Alexander's home was nestled at the heart, a stone's throw from Marlowe Castle. Because there was only one road leading out of the village, one might think it likely for one to glimpse Miss Finch out of the window as one's carriage rolled by.

One would be wrong.

There was no sign of her anywhere.

Alexander delivered the trunk without incident, then paused at the side of the road before climbing back into his carriage.

"I'll walk," he told his startled driver. "It's a beautiful day."

It was a ridiculously cold day. If it weren't for warm leather gloves and thick winter layers, he would have frozen into a ducal icicle the moment he'd stepped outside.

But mayhap a bit of fresh air would be good for him.

Alexander spent every Christmas here in Cressmouth, but never left his cottage. There was no time to. He was the host of a fortnight-long Yuletide party filled with activities that ran until three o'clock in the morning. Perhaps none of which required his presence after all.

Practically superfluous, his mother had said.

The two-mile hike back to the cottage uphill through the snow could take an hour. An hour in which he might *enjoy* his surroundings.

A snow-covered vista stretched in all directions as far as the eye could see. Marlowe Castle stood on the highest point, its towers and ramparts glistening where sunlight sparkled against snow and ice. Fields of evergreens rolled in every direction behind the castle, their spiky green needles shimmering beneath ice droplets that looked like crystals.

Once his carriage pulled away without him, Alexander stepped onto the pavement leading up toward the castle. The walking path was kept clear on both sides of the road, for the convenience of tourists.

Alexander had kept a country home here for

years, and never properly considered himself a tourist.

The blacksmith shop across the street bustled with business. Sleighs, carriages, and carts lined the road.

He was friends with the le Duc brothers who ran the shop. Sébastien, Lucien, and family attended Alexander's Christmas Day open house every year.

He had never been inside the blacksmith shop.

Was this his opportunity to change that?

Or was Alexander courting scandal by risking being glimpsed so far away from the party he was meant to be hosting?

He was already walking home, he reasoned. Pausing to greet a neighbor wouldn't be seen as a crime. Especially not in a village as friendly as Cressmouth.

Alexander picked his way across the road to the shop.

The le Duc brothers' Uncle Jasper greeted him with a smile. "Happy Christmas, Your Grace. Where's your carriage? We can't mend it if you don't bring it."

"My carriage is fine," Alexander assured him. "Happy Christmas to you, too."

"Well, if you're looking for the lads, they're inside playing billiards with their sister and Miss Finch. Difficult to say which team's winning the tournament."

Alexander stared at him.

Miss Finch was inside the blacksmiths' house.

Playing *billiards*.

"Go on back," said Jasper. "The door's un-locked. Billiard room is second on the right."

Which was how the Duke of Nottingvale found himself straightening his cravat and brushing snow from his lapels on the le Ducs' front step, before opening the door himself, since there was no servant to do it for him.

The loud *thwack* of colliding balls greeted him, followed by hoots of laughter. Even without Jasper's instructions, finding the billiard room would have been obvious.

Alexander placed his hat on a wooden rack, and after a moment's indecision added his coat as well.

He wasn't going to *stay*, but it would be rude to drip melting snow all over the house.

After taking an extra moment to stomp his boots onto a conveniently located rug, he raked his fingers through his hat-crushed hair and strode down the short corridor to the open doorway of the billiard room.

Miss Finch was bent over the table to take a shot, which gave Alexander a splendid view down her bodice at the soft bosom she'd pressed his hands into during his completely ill-thought-out game of charades.

She glanced up and smiled at him just as she took her shot.

Despite her inattention, the cue ball tapped smartly against two other balls, provoking groans from the two brothers.

"Unbelievable." Sébastien le Duc refilled his glass of champagne. "That was witchcraft, plain and simple. You ladies are unmitigated cheats."

Miss Finch wagged a finger at him. "Be careful. Those are dueling words."

"Don't do it," Désirée warned her brother. "Your top hat still has a hole in it from last time."

Alexander gaped at Miss Finch. "You *shot* him?"

"I shot his hat," she replied.

"You could have *killed* him," he sputtered.

"Often the stated purpose of a duel," Désirée pointed out.

"Doing so would've required skill indeed." Miss Finch grinned at Alexander unrepentantly. "Whenever we duel, we place our headwear at twenty paces and aim at that instead. You should have seen what this rotter's five-shot pepperbox did to my favorite bonnet."

"Whenever you duel," Alexander repeated faintly.

She held out her cue stick. "Here. You can take my next shot."

"*Non*," said Lucien. "It is men against women, *s'il te plaît.*"

Sébastien narrowed his eyes at Alexander. "Are you any good?"

"Horrid," Alexander admitted.

Sébastien waved him ahead. "Take all of Cynthia Louise's shots. *Please.*"

"May I ask what you're doing here?" Désirée enquired. "Aren't you supposed to be at your party?"

"I'm not staying," Alexander said quickly. "I'm just... I just..."

None of his motivations would satisfactorily explain his presence *here* and not *there*.

At least, nothing he wished to admit to.

"Of course you're staying," Miss Finch said as she placed the cue stick into his hands. "What's the point of being a duke if you can't roll about in the mud or perform circus tricks or wager at billiards with friends instead of attending your own party once in a while?"

"None of those are things dukes do," he informed her.

She smiled. "They should."

Sébastien motioned toward the green baize. "Take your shot."

Alexander frowned at the table. "Where did the pockets go?"

"*Mon Dieu*," Lucien muttered.

Sébastien chortled with glee. "This is the best thing that could have happened to this tournament. He's never seen carom billiards before!"

"What do I do?" Alexander whispered to Miss Finch.

She demonstrated. "With a straight rail, your cue ball hits both object balls in one strike."

He tried.

It did not work.

"My turn." Sébastien leapt to his feet. "Prepare for destruction."

Miss Finch handed Alexander an empty goblet. "Red or white wine?"

He set the goblet down. "Miss Finch—"

All three le Ducs stared at him. "You call her 'Miss Finch?'"

"As is proper," Alexander said.

More to the point, Miss Finch hadn't given him leave to call her anything else.

"I like it," announced Sébastien. "His Grace is

only permitted 'Miss Finch' whilst everyone else in the village may call her Cynthia Louise for short."

"'Miss Finch' is shorter than 'Cynthia Louise,'" Alexander pointed out defensively.

"And as a penalty for Sébastien's impudence," Miss Finch interrupted, "I hereby grant His Grace permission to call me 'Cynthia,' which is even shorter than 'Cynthia Louise.'"

"I thought we were friends," Sébastien muttered.

He and his siblings swiveled expectant gazes toward Alexander.

"Er," he said.

From the moment he'd inherited the title, no one outside of the family had ever again called Alexander by his Christian name.

His spine tingled as he said, "Miss—er—Cynthia may call me 'Alexander' whilst the rest of you scoundrels continue to call me 'Nottingvale.'"

"*Rude*," said Sébastien. "You're catching on."

He then bent to the table and made several shots that inspired grunts of approval from his brother and good-natured cursing from two very unladylike ladies.

Alexander should have been appalled.

Instead, he couldn't stop smiling.

He was having more fun than he had ever had at a Yuletide party, and all he'd done was walk into a room, fail to make his shot, and parry a few insults.

"Champagne," he decided. Rather than red or white wine, the moment definitely called for champagne.

Sébastien widened his eyes. "But England, she is at war with la France. Surely you do not accuse humble French immigrants of smuggling contraband from foreign soil."

"There's champagne in your glass," Désirée pointed out.

"So there is." Sébastien retrieved a bottle from the sideboard behind him and held the neck out toward Alexander. "Veuve Clicquot? 1811 was a comet vintage. You shan't be disappointed."

Cynthia Louise held out her glass as well, which caused the others to do the same.

"To Alexander and Cynthia!" cheered Désirée.

"Er," said Alexander.

His protest went unheard over the clinking of glasses.

Cynthia's blue eyes sparkled at him over the top of her champagne.

"Halt the tournament," she commanded. "Shall we at least teach Alexander the rules?"

"And some illegal shots, just for sport," Sébastien added.

Désirée nodded sagely. "So he knows what *not* to do."

The others laughed.

Alexander did not. He had always known what not to do.

Such as abandoning his own party.

Or playing drunken billiards at one o'clock in the afternoon.

Or granting a hoyden like Cynthia Louise Finch leave to abandon all propriety and refer to him as Alexander.

No, propriety had been abandoned long before

he walked through the door. Alexander was merely...

Complicating matters.

"Very well," he said. "Who wants to explain how to make a cannon?"

The next hour and a half passed in a blur of failed shots on Alexander's part, a series of utterly impossible-to-make shots that everyone *but* Alexander was able to achieve on the first try, and the uncorking of a second bottle of champagne.

He'd lost track of the time.

Spending a playful, spontaneous afternoon with Cynthia was fun.

She was fun.

And unpredictable.

And terrifying.

She made him want more moments like these.

If he had missed her before when she sneaked away for a few hours, he would now be able to think of nothing else but how much he would rather be wherever she happened to be, doing whatever she wanted.

He tried to memorize every moment, but it was impossible. There were too many, and they kept coming. Teasing banter across the table. The flirtatious look in her eyes when she bent to take a shot—or leaned over to willfully distract him from his.

But like all good things, this too must end.

He handed Lucien the cue stick. "I must return to my party."

"I'll go with you," Cynthia said. "I need to make certain Gertie is following orders."

"Take him out back to meet Chef," said Désirée.

Sébastien smirked. "Don't let him fall in."

"What...?" Alexander asked.

Once they were cloaked and hatted, Cynthia led him out of the house and around the side, rather than down the front walk to the street.

"They have a pet hog," she explained. "Named Chef."

That raised more questions than it answered.

"I don't care about Chef," he said.

"Oh, all right." She pivoted back toward the smithy.

He stopped her. For the moment, they were hidden from view.

She lifted her questioning gaze to his.

"Thank you," he said. "For letting me stay even though you didn't invite me. For making me feel welcome, and for... attempting... to teach me carom billiards."

"You do know," she said, "you can do this whenever you like."

"Drink too much champagne and cause you to lose your tournament?"

"Enjoy yourself," she corrected. "What's the point of being a duke if you never do anything you like?"

He was starting to wonder.

"There is one thing I'd like to do..." He lifted his hand to her cheek.

She arched a brow. "Then stop talking and do it."

He pulled his hat from his head and dipped under the brim of her bonnet to kiss her.

The wind disappeared, the icy temperature, the

snow. There was only her lips. Her heat. Her tongue.

He couldn't have her, no matter how much he liked her. He *knew* that.

But they could have this kiss.

It would have to be enough.

He lifted his head.

"Let me guess," she said wryly. "You have to go and choose a bride?"

He winced. This was not well done of him.

"They're all perfect," he admitted. "How does one decide between perfection?"

"Are they perfect for *you?*" She tilted her head. "What if you lowered your standards to someone *almost* perfect? Close enough so that you're not mortified to be married to her, but imperfect enough to be interesting and amusing and un-afraid to put life first."

He frowned. "I thought you wanted me to marry your cousin."

She snorted. "Gertie doesn't want to marry *you*. No offense."

"None taken," he said faintly, then changed his mind. "All offense taken. Why attend the Debu-tante Derby if she doesn't want to marry me?"

"She didn't *know* she didn't want to until she met you."

Now he should definitely be taking offense.

Instead, all he could do was rejoice. For now at least, there was nothing to stop Cynthia from kissing him.

He wrapped his arms about her midsection.

She laced her fingers behind his neck. "You scare Gertie. But you don't scare me."

"Nothing does, I suspect." He suckled her bottom lip. "You scare the devil out of me."

She grinned. "Good."

That was the last word spoken for several long minutes as Alexander kissed her with all of the hunger he'd kept locked deep inside.

He wished more than anything that he and Cynthia Louise could have more than stolen kisses.

But he was a duke, and despite her opinion on the matter, dukes were not always able to do as they pleased.

CHAPTER 9

*C*ynthia Louise stood atop the snow-covered peak behind Marlowe Castle and flung her arms open wide.

This was the panorama she'd been craving. Snow in every direction. Rolling fields of evergreens to the left, red-roofed cottages of Cressmouth to the right, and directly in front of her... the perfect spot to slide down the mountain on skis.

Blast it all, she should have brought them along, just in case her scouting adventure bore fruit. Although the slightly less steep section just beside it was often used for sledding, that wasn't the only criteria for a ski hill. She'd needed to ascertain the depth and consistency of the snow, and ensure it stretched over the entire area.

Luckily for her, a snowstorm earlier that month had set things up nicely. The difficult part was going to be convincing Gertie to come with her. Every time the earl took the extended family on holiday to Norway, Gertie had stayed resolutely indoors drinking chocolate rather than strap on what she referred to as "death sticks."

Seeing Cynthia bed-bound in leg traction *twice* over the years hadn't helped matters. No matter how much Cynthia tried to explain that the danger didn't come from the skis, but rather the riskiness of the tricks attempted by the rider.

Tricks were optional! Gertie could just coast! Cynthia would be right there!

Such arguments hadn't swayed Gertie in the least.

Indeed, it was a comment by Gertie's father that wrought the magic. Once he'd married the last chit off, said the earl, he was ridding the manor of *all* their paraphernalia—from the pianoforte to the skis.

Nothing made a prospect more enticing than the daunting realization one might never have such an opportunity again.

Tomorrow, Cynthia decided. Tomorrow, she would convince Gertie.

Today was for *Cynthia's* freedom.

She flung her arms out wide.

It wasn't just that she treasured these unstructured moments above all else. "Gadding about," as her uncle called it, allowed her to bump into old friends or wander into new adventures.

And now, it also allowed her to avoid the Duke of Nottingvale.

Alexander.

Her cheeks heated.

Sneaking off to explore the village's festivities alone allowed her to avoid *Alexander.*

His kisses were exquisite.

No woman in her right mind would wish to avoid a moment's pleasure in his embrace.

But the obvious spark between them wasn't the problem.

The fact that he was going to marry someone *else* was the problem.

She'd known that before she came. She hadn't cared back then.

Very well, yes, she had cared deeply, but she'd thought he was going to marry *Gertie*, who was Cynthia's favorite person. Since the duke never looked twice at Cynthia anyway, why not have him rescue her cousin?

But Gertie didn't want the duke.

Cynthia did.

And Alexander wanted someone—*anyone*—but Cynthia Louise.

The only way to avoid being hurt when he made his final duchess selection, was to avoid *him*. The less time they spent together, the lower the probability of her exceedingly foolish tendre developing into something deeper.

After all, Cynthia had a long history of falling in things.

What she had to avoid falling into was love.

She turned from the gorgeous, perfect-for-skis, unblemished, snow-covered slope and stepped... right into the Duke of Nottingvale's chest.

"Good heavens!" He grabbed her shoulders and hauled her toward the castle ramparts. "You were standing on the edge of a *cliff*. You could have slid right off!"

"I plan to," she informed him. "What are you

doing here? Shouldn't you be entertaining guests at your party?"

"You're a guest at my party," he reminded her. "And you're not there. I came to... chastise you."

"You're not there, either," she pointed out. "Consider your chastisement rebutted."

Alexander glowered at her. "Very well. I confess. I came to see what you were doing."

He also hadn't let go of her yet. If anything, he was holding her closer.

She felt in danger of losing her balance over a different type of cliff.

With skis, Cynthia hadn't minded getting hurt, because she knew she could win in the end.

With Nottingvale, the game was already over.

She swallowed. "How did you know I was here?"

"I didn't," he admitted. "Fortunately, people tend to notice when you pass by, which provided subtle clues to follow."

"Was it the chestnut cart?" she asked. "Children love it when I eat chestnuts from the air whilst juggling them."

"It was the archery targets," he informed her. "The competition apparently isn't until tomorrow, but a certain hoyden paid five quid to practice shooting today... and didn't hit a single hay mound."

"My hands were sticky," she protested. "That was after the chestnuts."

He *still* hadn't let go of her.

She was suddenly aware how protected their position was behind the castle. Ramparts to one side, a forest to the other... They were out-of-doors yet completely hidden from view.

Anything could happen.

"Well." He tilted his head, his voice a low, seductive purr. "Now that I'm here, what shall we do with ourselves?"

Cynthia knew what *she* was going to do.

She was going to show him how incompatible they were.

Once she proved they didn't suit, he would see their flirtation was as pointless as it was temporary.

She respected her heart too much to be nothing more than a man's passing fancy.

If the duke wished to procrastinate, he could take up a hobby.

Juggling chestnuts was nice. So was picking a blasted bride, so as to put the rest of the party out of their misery.

"We'll begin," she said briskly, "in the counting house." Cynthia lifted her arm to point up high at the tallest tower. "It's in the room at the top."

He gulped. "Let me guess... It's countless uneven flights up a narrow, winding, windowless staircase?"

"Oh, you've already seen it?" she said brightly. "If the idea bores you, go on back to the party."

"I'll go," he said quickly. "Lead the way."

Marvelous.

But they'd no sooner stepped beneath the castle archway and in through the open entrance doors when the duke stopped stock-still and gazed about in childlike wonder.

"It's incredible." His voice was hushed, his expression filled with awe. "The interior looks *new*."

"Mr. Marlowe renovated the castle a decade ago." Cynthia stared at the duke in befuddlement. "Have you never been *inside* the castle before?"

He shook his head. "I heard there were free refreshments for villagers, but I don't require charity. I have a French chef and a well-stocked kitchen."

"People don't come to the castle for *charity*," she began, then corrected herself. "I concede that free food and entertainment is one of the reasons *I* came the first time. But it's far from the only reason. Wealthy tourists pay the same to rent a suite with a view for a fortnight as they would renting a room for an entire year in London. People come because it's Christmastide here, all year round. This village is a family anyone can drop into whenever they please. Fellow strangers are just future friends. And yes, the free cakes are nice." She frowned at him. "Why do *you* come?"

"For Christmas," he assured her. "But I put it on myself. I'm in London most of the year for Parliament, then at my country estate the rest of the year, making up for lost time. I tend to arrive here toward the beginning of December, a week or so before my guests, so that I have time to prepare. I must be present during the party because I am the host. After the grand Twelfth Night farewell ball, the house clears on Epiphany, and I head back to London myself the following day to retake my seat in the House of Lords."

"Wait," she said. "This isn't just your first time inside the castle. You're saying you own a holiday home at a famous perpetual Yuletide tourist destination... that you've never actually seen?"

"I can see the castle from my windows," he told her. "Well, parts of it. I can see the towers and the wall."

"Come with me."

She hooked her elbow around his and dragged him past the lavish reception area to a dining hall as large as any palace ballroom. Tables filled every inch of space. Villagers and tourists alike filled the tables.

"Look," the duke said in surprise. "They're eating—"

"The same sort of meals your French chef prepares?" Cynthia said dryly. "This may come as a shock, but Marlowe Castle *also* has French chefs. As well as not-French chefs. The menu is extensive and changes fortnightly."

"Fortnightly?" Alexander's brows shot up. "How can an extensive menu change fortnightly during the winter? Nothing but evergreens grows for miles around."

She took him out through a side door and into an enormous glasshouse.

"Behold," she said. "The conservatory, half of which is dedicated to fruits, vegetables, and spices. Where do you think your French chef obtains the items he cooks for you in your kitchen?"

The duke gazed about in wonder. "This indoor 'garden' is as big as a park!"

"Wait until you hear about all of the activities at Marlowe Castle in *addition* to eating," she said. "The ballroom hosts assemblies every week. Guests come from all corners to enjoy the orchestras and the dancing. I'm sure you passed the amphitheatre on your journey in?"

"I did know about the theatre," he assured her. "I just haven't had a chance to—"

"Unless it's raining, there are performances every day of the week. Plays, musicals, choirs, operas, acrobats... It's not Drury Lane, but it's fabulously entertaining. Many of the villagers act on stage or play an instrument."

He grinned. "I'm surprised *you* haven't done so."

She stared at him.

He closed his eyes. "Of course you've done so."

"I played Maria in Twelfth Night three years running." She swept him out of the conservatory and into the brisk winter air. "Through these trees is a path leading down to the lake, which is currently frozen over and will remain so through March, making it the perfect spot for ice-skating."

His face briefly twisted.

She stopped walking and placed her gloved fists on her hips. "Are you afraid of heights *and* skates?"

"I'm not *afraid*," he said defensively. "I'm a duke with no heirs. I could die falling down twenty flights of stairs, and I could die sinking through a patch of ice that's *supposed* to hold my weight, but doesn't."

"And you could die if your French chef decides to poison you, or if a squirrel spooks your horses and your carriage rolls off of a bridge. We all eventually die, whether we want to or not. The question is how you want to *live*."

"I..." he said.

Whatever he'd been about to say vanished as the six-foot, fourteen-stone duke darted from the path in a futile attempt to hide behind a leaf-less sapling.

"Did you see a squirrel?" she whispered.

"People," he whispered back. "I thought I heard voices I recognized."

Ah. The one thing that scared His Grace more than thin ice and tall towers and steep cliffs: being caught on a public path in proximity to Cynthia Louise Finch.

Not insulting *at all*.

The voices indeed belonged to people, and without doubt at least one of them knew Notting-vale well: the Duke of Azureford and his new bride strolled up the winding path arm-in-arm.

"Cynthia Louise!" squealed the Duchess of Azureford, better known as Cynthia's childhood friend Carole. Because Houville was so close to Cressmouth, they'd seen each other at least monthly for decades.

The ladies bussed cheeks and the Duke of Azureford inclined his head to the Duke of Not-tingvale, who had wisely abandoned the spindly sapling he'd hoped would disguise him.

"I hear you're as terrible at billiards as I am," Azureford said with a chuckle.

"Wonderful." Nottingvale sent Cynthia a dark look. "I'm now being gossiped about."

"I didn't create the gossip," she informed him. "Or invite you to billiards."

"We're inviting you both," said the duchess. "Cynthia Louise has visited our new billiards room countless times, but it would be lovely to play with partners. Perhaps later this week?"

"Er," said Nottingvale.

"He's hosting a party," Cynthia explained. "Right now, at this very second."

He shot her an even darker look.

"Of course it's still going on," the duchess said with a shake of her head. "I don't know what I was thinking. Perhaps Epiphany, then? Once the guests have departed?"

"We'll let you know," Cynthia said quickly. "In fact, I'll drop by tomorrow for tea, and catch you up on the latest scandal broth."

At Nottingvale's startled look, she whispered, "I'll leave out the good bits."

His face flushed crimson.

"Well, then," said the duchess. "You two look... busy. We'll carry on. I'll see you tomorrow, Cynthia Louise!"

As soon as they disappeared from sight, Alexander groaned and rubbed his face. "I cannot possibly play couples' billiards."

"Why not?" She raised her brows. "Is there some way to die from it? Their rank is as high as yours, and they're perfectly respectable. Besides, you already played couples' billiards with me at the le Ducs' house."

"I didn't mean to," he said. "Everything that happened was an accident."

"Some of the best things in life happen by accident," she told him. "The others happen on purpose. For example, by saying 'yes' when friends invite you to visit them. Unless..."

"They're friends," Alexander said quickly. "I'm

not shy or a misanthrope. I just... always have something else I ought to be doing. If I say yes to them, I'll have to say yes to everyone who asks, and then I'll never have time to attend to my responsibilities."

"Actually, no," Cynthia said. "I receive far more invitations than I could possibly accept. I am indescribably talented at accepting only the best ones, and sending polite regrets to the others. 'Polite regrets,'" she informed him, "are generally more socially acceptable than hiding behind a tree."

"In your circles," he muttered.

"What you need," she said, "is to separate the 'duke' from the 'duty.' One is a thing you *are*, and the other is a thing you *do*. Sometimes. When it fits in your calendar. Not all of the time, such as when you should be sleeping or relaxing."

"There's no time for relaxing," he said.

"Then you're doing the 'duke' bit wrong. Don't you have a secretary?"

"Yes, but—"

"And a man of business?"

"Yes, but—"

"And presumably an entire army of bankers and solicitors to manage the piles of gold in your coffers?"

"A team of five," he said. "And I wouldn't claim 'piles' of—"

"Alexander, you *can* live. You *should* live. I don't know who told you that your worth comes from working yourself to the bone attending to every detail yourself, but they lied. Your duty is to ensure the important things are accomplished. Disregarding your own needs isn't *virtuous*. It'll send you to an early grave." She poked at his chest. "*That's* what you should be afraid of."

He stared at her for a long moment.

"I *am* afraid of that," he said. "I'm afraid of not doing my duty. I'm afraid of doing nothing but my duty. I'm afraid of taking time for myself only to discover I no longer know who that is."

"Find out," she said softly. "Let yourself try. At the least, being less tightly wound will help you terrify fewer debutantes."

He sent her a flat look.

She grinned at him and smoothed his lapel. "It's an excellent experiment. If being New Relaxed Nottingvale helps you to woo your bride, it's practically an act of charity. You owe it to your future duchess to have less of a stick up your—" She cleared her throat into her fist.

"I thought the phrase was 'stick-in-the-mud,'" he said drily.

"I changed the words," she murmured.

He frowned. "Do you really think I'm boring and fusty?"

"No," she said. "I think *you* think that. Some well-intentioned goose told you a duke is nothing but constant duty, and you've convinced yourself duty is all you're good for. It's not true, Alexander. You can be a good duke, a good friend, a good kisser, and a terrible billiards player all at the same time."

His gaze heated. "A good kisser?"

"A mediocre kisser," she said. "Actually, I cannot even recall your kisses. I forget them at once, and don't want you to feel bad for not making much of an impression—"

He shut her up by whirling her behind the trees and covering her mouth with his.

Very well, she hadn't forgotten a single detail about his kisses. They were melting, searing deliciousness that haunted her dreams and caused her skin to tickle with gooseflesh every time his eyes met hers.

She wrapped her arms about his neck and kissed him back.

There was no winning this game. She knew she couldn't keep him. But maybe it was all right to pretend, just for this fortnight.

As long as she was careful to remember that kissing was just kissing, she could keep the armor around her heart intact.

He broke the kiss and rested his forehead against hers with obvious reluctance. "The sun is setting. I have to return to the party."

"I'll go with you," she said. "I have to check on Gertie."

"What are your plans for tomorrow?"

"I've a date to gossip about you behind your back at four o'clock."

"Before that," he amended.

"Hmm." She pretended to think it over. "I have a party I was planning not to attend."

"Excellent," he said. "I'll go with you."

She bit her lip to hide a wicked smile. "Only if you agree to do any activity of my choosing."

"I'm going to regret this," he muttered. "But yes. Anything."

Cynthia kissed him.

Tomorrow, he would truly live.

CHAPTER 10

*C*ynthia Louise tried not to giggle as the Duke of Nottingvale's skis bumped hers for the twentieth time as they smuggled the long wooden runners out through the rear servants' exit.

"I've never sneaked out of my own house before." Alexander had looked bewildered all morning. "You're a bad influence."

"I'm a terrible influence," she agreed cheerfully. "It's the best thing about me."

Fortunately, the close proximity of the duke's cottage to the castle meant they could hike up through the woods rather than conspicuously lug skis up the primary public road.

She had been disappointed but unsurprised when her cousin Gertie refused to take her still new skis for a practice slide. The idea had sent her straight into her burlap sack.

Cynthia had been delighted and *very* surprised when the Duke of Nottingvale had agreed to the adventure. He had stuck by her side all morning.

She slanted him a suspicious look. "Are you

doing this because you made the mistake of agreeing to 'anything' yesterday, and now feel it's your ducal duty to honor your word?"

"No. I meant 'anything.'" His brown eyes held hers. "I wanted to spend time with you."

Oh.

Very well, then.

No more questions.

With her cheeks flushing with heat, Cynthia averted her gaze to the woods and pointed at a nearby break in the evergreens. "There. That's our entrance to the castle."

"How did you know?" He narrowed his eyes. "Have you sneaked through my servants' access door before?"

She laughed, neither confirming nor denying the accusation. "I know because the only trick is to keep going *up*. The castle is at the top of the mountain and so is our launching-off point."

"Launching off," the duke repeated. "This plan sounds worse by the second."

"You can stay at the bottom of the hill and watch me have all of the merriment," she offered.

"No." His voice was low, and his gaze hot. "I absolutely intend to have fun *with* you."

She gave him a saucy grin and sauntered ahead, in part because the path through the trees was plenty narrow for one person to manage whilst balancing skis on her shoulder, and partly because...

Well, because she adored spending time with him, too.

Cynthia was used to people finding her spontaneous and unpredictable, but she'd never imagined feeling the same way about the Duke of Nottingvale.

No matter how many times she poked at him or how far he ventured from his usual comfort level, he remained a constant good sport; agreeable and easy-going. If he *hadn't* been born anchored to a dukedom, who knew what manner of antics he might have got up to?

Without that deuced dukedom, they might even have become more than friends.

Very well, they were more than friends. Or different from friends, anyway.

There wasn't really a word to describe two people who were completely wrong for one another, yet delighted in each other's company and indulged in forbidden kisses because they couldn't stay away from each other.

She suspected the only reason they weren't kissing at this moment was because of the six-foot skis forcing them to keep a respectable distance.

For now.

Her poles were in her other hand, and she used them to brush stray branches aside as they climbed through the woods.

Alexander's home was as close to the castle as possible without being inside its ramparts, but the thick snow and steep incline had them both breathing heavily by the time they burst through the trees up to the clear mountain peak.

"See?" she huffed as she rested her skis on the snow. "Going down will be positively *relaxing*."

Alexander sent her a dark look rather than dignify her comment with a response.

She led him around the ramparts, away from

the woods, to the spot she'd scouted the day before.

"Step one," she announced. "Arrange your skis just so."

His attention was riveted on her, and he copied her movements minutely.

"Step two," she said. "Climb on."

He stared down at his skis doubtfully.

She sank to her knees and lightly tapped the back of his muscular calf. "Come on, I'll strap you in."

"You're kneeling on snow," he said. "Aren't your legs freezing?"

"They would be," she agreed, "if I weren't wearing buckskin trousers beneath my gown and petticoats."

"Of course you are," he muttered.

But he lifted each of his boots with obvious trepidation and placed his feet atop the skis.

She made quick work of the leather straps, ensuring the fit was secure and snug before adjusting his grip on his poles.

They spent the next half an hour going over how to steer, how to stop, and how to fall safely if necessary.

"Where did you learn this again?" he asked.

"Norway," she reminded him. "We have relatives who live there. My cousin Olaf is a captain in the Cadastre Corps. Did you know that the Scandinavian military has trained with skis for over one hundred years?"

"I did not," the duke said faintly.

"Of course, Scandinavian farmers and hunters had already been using skis for centuries," she explained. "For the Corps, it was all very practical. Military drills over rough terrain, cross-country journeys on skis, target practice whilst on skis, and so on. Until Olaf decided to do something *im*practical."

"A cousin of yours did something impractical?" Alexander murmured. "I am agog with shock."

She grinned at him. "He launched himself ten feet into the air, flying over the dumbfounded gazes of his fellow soldiers. He was instantly infamous, and only became more talented and daring after that. He's the one who taught me everything I know."

"Wonderful," said the duke. "I feel so much safer. Didn't you break your leg? Twice?"

She wiggled her eyebrows. "And I won a two-hundred-pound wager."

"Two... hundred..."

She adjusted her poles. "Ready?"

"I am not ready. I will never be ready." He took a deep breath. "But here we go."

He turned away from her and braced his poles.

She grabbed his arm and hauled him back to her side.

"Not that direction. The village is down there. I aimed our skis over here for a reason." She gestured down with her gloved hand. "This section runs parallel to the sledding path. There are no obstructions, and people already know to keep a safe distance at the bottom."

He looked shaken. "I almost skated into the village?"

"You probably would have slid face-first into a

haystack and had straw falling out of your hair for days."

"What if I veer too far the other direction?"

"Just point your skis straight down. You won't have to steer. Honestly, this section is so wide, you can't possibly run into anything. Except me, I suppose. But I skate well enough on skis to steer clear of danger."

"Except for two broken legs."

"Those were my first two attempts!"

"Your first two attempts to ski involved jumping from one cliff to another?" he said in disbelief. "No. Don't tell me. I have just learned an important lesson about never again volunteering to 'do anything' with Miss Cynthia Louise Finch."

"You'll adore it," she promised him. "It feels like flying. It's my favorite thing, and I've never had anyone in England to share it with." She gave him a shy smile. "I'm glad it's with you."

"Oh, very good," he said. "Now my brain is full of kissing you, instead of imagining all of the ghastly ways this plan could go horribly awry."

She grinned at him. "I'll let you kiss me at the bottom."

Before he could reply, she pushed with her poles and sailed down the side of the mountain.

It was glorious.

The sun dazzled her eyes and the wind whipped tendrils of hair from her chignon. Her skis were fast and smooth. Cynthia had waxed them that morning, just as Olaf had taught her.

All too soon, she reached the plateau. She twisted her legs sharply, turning to watch the

Duke of Nottingvale's progress down the mountain.

He was... not smooth.

His skis went every direction but straight, sometimes touching in the front, sometimes touching in the back.

Rather than guide the poles, his arms windmilled for balance, tipping him precariously one direction, then another.

The expression on his face was alternately terrified and exhilarated, as if every moment he remained upright was a victory in its own right.

He looked absolutely magnificent.

And he was headed in her direction.

"Stop," she called out. "Turn your skis to break the velocity."

The duke's skis did nothing of the sort.

He flailed his arms wilder.

Cynthia scooted several quick steps to one side.

As he skated past, she grabbed hold of his arm. The sudden check spun his momentum toward her. Their skis tangled, followed by their legs, and their arms, and a collision of chests.

In the space of a heartbeat, she was flat on her back with the Duke of Nottingvale splayed on top of her, both of them winded and panting.

He kissed her hard.

"That... was... *brilliant*." His eyes sparkled. "Let's do it again!"

She let go of her poles and wrapped her arms about him. "I thought you wanted a kiss."

He covered her face with kisses. "Can you teach me to jump crevasses?"

She closed her eyes and groaned. "I've spawned a monster."

"It's definitely your fault." He kissed her again. "Everything good is."

He'd let go of his poles, too. One hand was cradling her head, whilst the other propped him at an angle in an attempt not to crush her.

It was the least comfortable position she had ever been in, and an experience she would cherish for the rest of her life. She kissed him as though there might never be another chance.

At last, she pushed him aside.

"Too many kisses?" he asked. "Do I have to skate down again to earn another?"

No. He could have all of the kisses he desired.

"Let me unfasten these before we break a ski or an ankle." She fumbled with the leather straps, then piled the skis and the poles to one side. "*Now* we can roll around in the snow like mature, responsible adults."

He grinned and flipped onto his back, bringing her with him so that she was splayed on top of him.

"My heart won't stop racing." His smile was the widest she'd ever seen. "It's either from proximity to you or my near-death experience."

"Definitely the skis," she assured him.

"I'm not so sure." His eyes were unreadable.

He held her gaze for a long moment, then cupped her head and drew her mouth down to his.

Now it was her heart that wouldn't stop racing. Either from proximity to him... or the realization that she never wanted to let him out of her sight.

Even if they never had another moment like this again.

What if they stayed friends after this? What if she saw him not once a year at Christmastide, but on planned holidays all year long? Would she be able to withstand the sight of him building a life with his new bride?

Would she be able to stand not seeing him at all?

"Come on, then." She rolled from his chest and to her feet, then bent to offer him her hand. "Shall we see what you might earn after your *second* slide down the mountain?"

They picked up their equipment and trudged over to the tree line to begin the hike back up to the top.

"I cannot believe these are Lady Gertrude's skis," he murmured.

"Gertie will *never* use them," Cynthia replied drily. "They're the Duke of Nottingvale's skis now."

"Isn't it bad form to give away someone else's possessions?"

"Isn't it bad form to skate down a mountain-side strapped to someone else's possessions?"

"Touché. My skis. I'm happy to pay her for them."

"I'd rather you introduce her to a young, single, eligible gentleman with deep pockets, an old title, a kind heart, and a penchant for pianoforte music."

"Hmm." They kept walking. "Well... there's me."

"You're not young," she reminded him. "You're a spinster like me."

He snorted. "No one thinks of you as a spinster."

"*Everyone* thinks of me as a spinster. I have only to enter your ballroom and the mothers' whispers begin at once."

"Ah, well, I meant 'no one with any sense.' But I do see your point. Lady Gertrude is eighteen years, one month, and... let me count... nine days old."

Cynthia giggled. "She regaled you with a few choice facts?"

"All of the facts," he assured her. "I am now a Lady Gertrude expert. Which of the previous qualities you mentioned are the ones she seeks?"

"Penchant for pianoforte music," Cynthia replied without hesitation. "Gertie would marry an actual pianoforte if she could."

The duke was silent for a moment. "Why not let her?"

"I don't... know if you know this," Cynthia said slowly, "but pianofortes have a difficult time walking down wedding aisles in the local chapel."

"I don't mean literally marry one. But if she'd rather have music than a husband, why not let her, at least for a little while? She's only eighteen. She has at least thirty-six more months before she turns irrevocably dusty and unmarriageable."

"I would do so," Cynthia said with feeling, "if it were up to me. Unfortunately, the only person with any say in the matter is Gertie's father. The earl has decreed he will marry off his final daughter in January, come what may. Either *I* match her to deep pockets and a coronet, or her father will hand her off to a roué three times her age."

"I see." Alexander was silent for a moment. "I'll make a few inquiries."

"You will?" she said in surprise.

They exited the trees and emerged back atop the peak.

He turned to face her. "Why wouldn't I? If it's in my power to avert what sounds like a lifetime of misery for Lady Gertrude, then of course I'll do my best to find her a match she can live with."

A weight lifted from Cynthia's chest.

"Thank you," she said with a grateful smile. "It will be a Christmas miracle."

"Shall I make inquiries for you as well?"

The smile slid from her face.

The duke was trying to be kind, not cruel, she reminded herself. He might kiss her at every opportunity, but they both knew those opportunities would soon end. He had never tried to mislead her. She'd understood the situation long before her lips first met his.

"I'm on the shelf," she said tightly.

He shrugged. "People remove things from shelves all of the time."

She stared at him, then swallowed.

"I'm not the right fit for the people in your echelons, and we both know it."

If she hadn't been right twelve years ago when she was a bundle of girlish nerves trying her very, very best... then she definitely wasn't right now.

There was a *reason* he'd hid behind a tree rather than be seen with her. Cynthia could harm Alexander's standing just by existing next to him.

Just being in her vicinity was embarrassing.

The unwelcome reminder sapped much of the joy out of the day.

"Come on." She positioned his skis. "I'll strap you in."

Once his skis were safely attached, she attended to her own.

She gestured toward the sledding slope. "Remember, we skate in this direction. Over there is—"

"The village," he said. "I remember."

Not just the village.

Gertie.

Cynthia's mouth fell open.

Max gave a loud yip.

"You *are* using the skis!" Gertie squealed. "I saw they were missing, and I wanted to watch. Can I watch?"

"Stay next to the wall!" Cynthia commanded. "It's slippery here, and I don't need you breaking your neck."

"There was a higher probability of neck-breaking if you'd talked me into those skis," Gertie replied, cradling Max to her chest. "From the look of things, you haven't fared much better. You two have snow *everywhere*."

"Er," said the Duke of Nottingvale.

"Er," said Cynthia.

"Well, make haste," said Gertie. "They think I'm taking Max for a walk, but I can't stay long. Max loves the snow and keeps getting lost in it. I only find him when I see his little tail poking out. He's angry at me for carrying him up this mountain. You'd think the snow was hiding a field of bones to chew—"

At the word *bones*, Max yipped and sprung himself from Gertie's chest.

He did not get lost in the snow.

He tumbled backward down the slick mountain, his yip turning to terror as he slid off the incline and over the edge—in the wrong direction.

"Dammit, Max," Cynthia muttered, and pushed off after him.

This direction wasn't as smooth as the other, and bumps beneath the snow sent her skis a few inches into the air before continuing on with a jarring thud.

Max was tumbling out of control now, a spinning, howling, puppy-avalanche of white snow and brown fur.

He wasn't headed into the heart of the village.

He was headed straight for the area blocked off at the base of the castle... for the archery tournament.

Which was currently in progress.

"Damn it, Max!" she shouted, but of course he couldn't hear her, not that he could do anything about it if he did.

The poor terrified puppy shot down the mountain like a cannonball.

Right into the line of fire.

Cynthia sucked in a breath.

The terrain grew almost too bumpy to navigate the closer she drew to the targets. She was carried forward by pure speed and velocity rather than talent.

With a final yip, Max thudded into the base of one of the haystacks.

He didn't move.

"*Damn it, Max.*" Her throat pricked with heat. "Do *not* die."

She was seconds away.

Possibly seconds too late.

She passed both poles to her left hand and hunkered down to scoop up the non-moving puppy as she whisked them both out of danger.

He made a tiny mewling sound and shuddered against her chest.

"Thank God." She pressed her lips to his icy, matted fur. "We almost—"

And then fire ripped through her shoulder.

CHAPTER 11

The moment Cynthia took off after the puppy, Alexander took off after Cynthia.

He had no idea what he was doing.

This side of the mountain was nowhere near as smooth as the other, and he hadn't been graceful on the easy slope. It took all his effort to maintain his balance as gravity did most of the work hurtling him down the mountainside after Cynthia.

He wasn't as skilled as her.

He wasn't as fast as her.

He had to watch in horror as he realized the haystacks she'd mentioned earlier were the targets set up for the archery tournament. Right in front of them.

Eighty yards away.

Sixty yards away.

Alexander winced as the puppy slammed into the base of a target and stopped moving.

Cynthia was there instantly, her knees bent and her back straight and her poles tucked to one side as she ducked down and scooped up the puppy as though the rescue maneuver came as natural as yawning.

She was the most amazing creature he had ever seen.

A guardian angel. A—

Thwack.

Cynthia lurched upward, all her grace gone. She jerked backward, with a long wooden rod protruding from her chest.

Terror ripped through Alexander's veins like a flash fire.

Cynthia fell to the ground, motionless, the little brown puppy clutched in her arms.

"No!" he roared, not caring who heard him. He flew forward on panic alone.

He was going to kill all of the archers.

Right after he reached Cynthia's side.

Twenty yards.

Ten.

His skis caught on who-knew-what and Alexander went sprawling, landing in an ungainly heap two haystacks down from hers.

People were running toward them.

They were still a hundred yards away.

He flung his poles aside and threw off his skis, half sprinting, half scrambling, across the ice-slick snow. He gathered Cynthia up and cradled her to his chest.

"I will kill you if you die," he choked into her hair.

"Ironic," she mumbled. "I like it."

She was alive.

"I didn't mean to!" came a panicked, desperate voice.

"Is that... the Duke of Nottingvale?" said another.

Alexander didn't let go of Cynthia.

He wasn't certain he ever could.

"If you take one step closer," he snarled at the adolescent lad with the tear-stained face, "I will rip you asunder with my bare hands."

The lad blanched and nodded jerkily, new tears escaping to join the others.

"Is she... dead?" he stuttered.

"She's alive." The look of abject relief on the boy's face matched Alexander's own. "Go and summon a doctor."

The lad nodded and ran off, his thin elbows spiking into the air.

Alexander lowered his mouth to Cynthia's matted temple.

"If you die..." he growled.

"You'll kill me," she mumbled. "I remember."

"What the devil were you thinking?" His body still hadn't stopped shaking. Might never stop shaking.

"It was Max," she protested weakly.

A pathetic mewl sounded from the direction of her bodice.

"I got him," she whispered.

"I don't care about Max." His body was definitely never going to stop shaking. "I've got *you*."

"If it makes you feel better," she said tentatively. "I think it's a flesh wound."

"It does not make me feel better. It makes me feel like throttling you."

"I think I could walk. If you let go of me."

"You are not going to walk. There is an arrow

sticking out of you. I am going to carry you home and possibly everywhere else if that's what it takes to keep you safe."

She tugged at the wooden rod.

It didn't come loose.

Alexander's stomach roiled.

"Stop that," he snapped.

"It's not deep in me," she said. "At least, not all of the way in. I think part of it is stuck on my petticoats."

"Don't touch it. I'll summon every doctor for miles and they'll sort out the right thing to do."

"You know..." Her voice was faint, and her head lolled against his chest. "Maybe I can't walk."

"Damn it, Cynthia Louise!" He held her tighter, his throat tight. "You *must* stop acting as though your life doesn't matter. I have a duty to my title, but you have a duty to the entire world. We would all be much poorer without Miss Cynthia Louise Finch."

He lifted her up and stumbled down the road toward his cottage with half of the village trailing close behind.

"What about the skis?" she murmured.

"I don't give a damn about the skis."

The arrow wobbled with each step, making Alexander's stomach churn in protest. It was not protruding from her chest, as he'd first feared, but rather from her shoulder.

Blood had seeped through all her layers of clothing to blossom around the arrow like a red rose of death.

"It looks like you'll miss tea with the duchess," he informed her.

"Don't worry," she mumbled. "Carole will definitely hear this gossip."

He didn't doubt that.

People appeared to be pouring from their houses to fall into step around them. Oswald had the door flung wide long before Alexander lurched up the path. His footmen spilled out of the open doorway and dashed up to him with matching expressions of alarm.

They held out their arms. "Can we—"

"*No*," Alexander growled, muscling past them.

All of the female guests were packed into the entryway.

His mother stood front and center.

"What is the meaning of this?" demanded the duchess.

"There's an arrow sticking out of her," he said icily. "I'm trying to stop that."

"Where were you?" stammered one of the debutantes.

"Skating down the mountain on skis," one of the villagers replied helpfully.

The crowd immediately began talking over each other at once to recount the vivid tale of the archery contest, and the dog, and the lady on skis, who bravely rescued the dog, and the duke on skis, who then rescued *her*.

"You absented yourself from your own party," the duchess bit out each syllable, "to play on *skis* with... this creature?"

"He saved my life," Cynthia croaked out. "He's a hero. He's still marriageable. Go back to charades."

The duchess's voice was glacial. "You're in his *arms*."

"Pretend *this* is charades?" Cynthia offered in a small voice.

"*Move*," Alexander growled. "All of you."

The crowd parted, but barely.

"He's here!" cried a voice from just outside the door.

The lad who had shot Cynthia with his bow and arrow skidded into the entranceway, wild-eyed and breathing fast.

"He's here," he repeated, pointing behind him. "The doctor's here."

"Good." Alexander headed into the corridor. "You two can follow me."

CHAPTER 12

*L*ady Gertrude burst through the bedchamber door just as Alexander was easing his arm out from under Cynthia Louise so Doctor Quinney could inspect her.

"Gertie," Cynthia croaked, her voice faint. "I got Max."

Lady Gertrude burst into tears and crumpled beside the bed with her face pressed into the blanket.

"I'm sorry," she sobbed. "I shouldn't have gone. I shouldn't have taken Max. I should've held on tighter. I—"

"It's not your fault," said the lad. "I'm the one who shot her."

Lady Gertrude whirled from the bed to her feet like a wild tempest. She was across the bedchamber in seconds.

The slap reverberated around the room.

The lad didn't dodge the blow, nor flinch when it landed.

"I'm sorry," he said. "I deserved that. I didn't see her or the dog. I was concentrating on the target, and as soon I released my arrow... She slid right into it. I wished it had doubled back and hit me instead."

Lady Gertrude's lip wobbled. "That's how I felt, too."

"Well!" The sound of the duchess's loud sniff filled the doorway. "I don't see how it's at all appropriate to have not one, but two unrelated men in the sickroom whilst the doctor—"

"*You*," Alexander commanded the white-faced lad. "Take Lady Gertrude to the parlor, where Her Grace is about to serve hot tea."

"But Vale," the duchess stammered, her eyes wide with shock. "We—"

"—will speak once the doctor has concluded his examination." Alexander raised his brows pointedly. "A maid shall stay for propriety's sake. As to the rest of you: *Goodbye*."

Lady Gertrude hurried out of the room with the lad close behind her.

He shut the door tight.

Good boy.

"Now what?" Alexander asked the doctor.

"Now we cut away these clothes." Doctor Quinney sent Cynthia an apologetic expression. "I'm sorry, young lady. The arrow is stuck. Besides, I cannot take the risk of your wound ripping worse just to save garments that are already ruined."

Stuck arrow.

Wound ripping.

Alexander sat down hard on the dressing stool. The guest chamber went gray at the edges of his vision.

Doctor Quinney kept up a cheerful patter as he sliced through Cynthia's layers to expose her shoulder. He paused before he cut over her chest.

"Shall we ask His Grace to exit the room?" he asked softly.

"He can stay," Cynthia croaked. "I was going to show him my bosom anyway."

Alexander covered his fire-red face with one hand.

"She's jesting," he assured the doctor.

"You slid down on skis a second time." She gave Alexander a wobbly smile. "I promised you'd earn *something*."

"Whereas you," said the doctor, "took an arrow for your efforts. Fortunately, the trajectory was impeded by your thick coat and so many layers. The arrowhead came out cleanly, and the torn flesh will only require a few stitches."

Arrowhead.

Torn flesh.

Alexander dropped his head between his knees and tried to breathe.

Cynthia's tremulous voice sounded amused. "Is the big strong duke afraid of a little bit of blood?"

"I never was before," he mumbled. "But when it's you..."

"A funny phenomenon that happens all of the time," said the doctor with a chuckle. "Nurses who tend horrific battle wounds discover they cannot withstand the tiniest cut on their child's finger, all because it's someone they love."

All because of someone they love.

"No," Alexander rasped. "Dukes are not ruled

by romantic emotions. Mayhap I've just turned into a coward."

Cynthia Louise closed her eyes.

"Mayhap you have," replied the doctor cryptically. "Will you ring for boiling water and fresh towels? I have needle and thread in my satchel."

Needle and thread.

Alexander sprang up from the dressing stool and dashed to the wall to tug the bell pull.

It was answered immediately.

"Your Grace?"

"Boiling water," Alexander barked. "Fresh towels." He suddenly remembered Max. "And... a hot bath and clean blankets."

The maids nodded and bobbed and scurried away.

He approached the bed with caution.

Doctor Quinney was holding a thick square of gauze to the wound, hiding it momentarily from sight.

Alexander lifted the wet, shivering lump of fur from the middle of the bed.

"Max is sorry, too," Cynthia said. "It's been a long day for all of us."

"I'm going to give him a bath," Alexander said gruffly. "And then perhaps Doctor Quinney can glance over him once he's finished attending you."

A knock sounded at the door.

When Alexander answered, maids poured in with fresh towels and boiling water for the doctor, followed by a pair of footmen carrying a hot bath for Max. Another maid hurried in behind them bearing soap and blankets.

"Thank you," Alexander said before shooing them all back out.

Attending Max would give him something else to concentrate on besides Doctor Quinney's needle in Cynthia's arm.

"The duchess is upset," she said.

"Don't talk to me while he's sewing you," he answered.

Barely a heartbeat passed before she spoke again.

"I'll tell her you weren't with me."

"Doctor Quinney can hear you conspiring." Alexander gently soaped Max's fur in the warm water. "And everyone saw you with me. As my mother pointed out, you were in my arms."

"But I didn't begin that way. Everyone saw that, too. I'll say you rescued me while I was out with Gertie. They'll have no problem believing me a terrible chaperone. Today needn't interfere with your plans of finding a respectable bride."

He ground his teeth.

She was right. He *needed* a respectable bride. His duties to his title and his mother and his future heirs had not changed.

But what he wanted was someone like Cynthia Louise.

"No," he said. "You were brave and heroic and I'm not going to hide that."

"And foolhardy?" she said timidly.

"And foolhardy," he agreed. "I am still going to throttle you."

"No throttling," said the doctor. "Those stitches must remain clean and safe for a fortnight."

"And then I can throttle her?" Alexander said with amusement.

"By then, you won't remember you wanted to." The doctor crossed the room and held out his hands for the puppy. "Let me see this fellow."

Alexander placed the blanket-clad puppy in the doctor's arms and hurried to Cynthia's side.

"You were going to show me your bosom?" he whispered.

"No," she whispered back. "It was an empty bribe to lure you down the hill."

"You didn't tell me the bribe," he pointed out. "I don't think it was empty at all. I think there was a bosom in my future, until that blasted puppy ruined the moment."

She batted her eyelashes. "You'll never know."

Yes. That was exactly the problem.

Now he'd never know.

"Well, your puppy is bruised and sore," announced the doctor, "but he'll be fine. As for you, young lady, I'm leaving a few drops of laudanum in a small bottle on the table. Keep the wound clean and dry, and only take the laudanum if you must. If you return home before the wound has healed, please have a doctor attend to the stitches."

She nodded.

Alexander stood. "Thank you, Doctor Quinney. I'll see that you're well compensated for this visit."

"You're leaving the sickroom with me," said the doctor. "Our patient needs to rest. And it is perhaps not best for Your Grace to be alone with Miss Finch, if your bride is on the other side of this door."

Mortifying.

And true.

The bride business was only one problem. Cynthia's reputation was at stake as well.

She was barely accepted as it was, due to her outrageous antics, but Alexander had never heard a whisper of gossip about her allowing some cad to take liberties.

He was the cad.

The doctor was right.

It was time to go.

When he stepped out into the corridor, he expected the flock to surround him with questions at once.

No one approached.

"The patient will survive," said the doctor. "She'll have a nice scar, but..." His eyes met Alexander's. "She's free to leave when she likes."

"*I'd* like to leave," said one of the debutantes with tears swimming in her eyes. "We came here to spend Christmastide with the duke, but he'd rather not spend it with *us*."

Murmurs of agreement rippled through the crowd.

Superb.

Independent of the bride hunt, Alexander had hoped to provide all of his guests a very merry holiday... and instead had ruined their Yuletide.

"Nottingvale was gone for two hours," his sister Belle said firmly. "He has spent every other moment from dawn to... well, to dawn again, ensuring your comforts and providing your entertainment. One can hardly begrudge my brother a moment's rest—"

"He wasn't *resting*," said one of the mothers. "He was sliding down a mountain on skis."

Fair point.

Alexander appreciated his sister's support, but even she had to see the gaping hole in her logic.

"We're leaving," said another mother. "If this is how His Grace comports himself when he's *trying* to win our favor, then he is not the sort of 'gentleman' my daughter should marry."

"I apologize," he said quickly. "Nothing untoward occurred—"

"Besides spending the day unchaperoned in the company of woman who later turns up with an arrow sticking out of her chest?"

"Besides that," Alexander muttered.

He'd never had to make excuses before. His behavior had always been perfect.

"If you two are leaving," said another mother, "we're leaving, too."

Alexander's muscles froze.

A beat of silence filled the entryway.

"So are we," said one of the chaperones.

"Us, too," said another.

"Ooh," whispered one of the debutantes to her friend, "this is going to be in *all* of the scandal sheets by morning."

"We're going to be *so* popular," her friend whispered back.

Wonderful.

Splendid.

Everything was going exactly to plan.

Alexander wished there were some way to begin this day all over again.

"Of course it was *her* who caused the trouble," one of the mothers said with a sniff. "The moment she arrived, we should all have turned around and left."

"Miss Finch caused no trouble," Alexander said firmly. "Her puppy was in danger, and she saved its life."

"The mongrel wouldn't have *been* in danger," said another, "if it didn't belong to Miss Finch."

"And *you*." Face stricken, one of the chaperones turned toward Alexander's mother. "Men will be... *men*, but one expects more from the Duchess of Nottingvale. You are the hostess of this party. Everything that occurs under this roof is your responsibility."

"You will leave her out of this discussion," Alexander thundered. "My mother is innocent in this matter. My actions are my responsibility alone."

"And he didn't do them under this roof," Belle added.

He slanted her a furious glance to *stop helping*.

"She's right," said another. "Her Grace informed us you would be choosing a bride at this gathering, and clearly your attentions are elsewhere. We came here under false pretenses."

"You came to a Yuletide party," said Alexander. "It's Yuletide. I host this party every year, and the primary *raison d'être* has always been Christmas. I do intend to choose a bride, but I did hope the festivities would be amusing for all."

Mother's face was pale, but kept her spine ramrod straight and her chin tilted upward.

Alexander hadn't just created his own mess.

He'd caused his mother's friends to turn on her, too.

"Come along, Sally," said one of the mothers. "We're leaving."

Alexander kept his spine rigid. Between his scandal and Belle's, their once-perfect family was now a liability. This was more than just a disruption in a party. Acquaintances would now need to decide if they still wished to associate with them. Their return to London next week would be cold indeed.

"Tea will be served in the red parlor in forty-five minutes," Belle told the dispersing guests.

"How many do you think will be there?" he asked once the entranceway had emptied.

His sister winced. "Half?"

"The worst half," said their mother. "The grasping social climbers and grubby fortune hunters."

Alexander frowned. "You selected the guest list. I thought all these women were your friends."

"Not anymore," she said bitterly. "Perhaps they never were."

Belle looked as horrified as Alexander felt.

They had never seen their mother *doubt* before.

The duchess had always been strong and sure. Imperious. Occasionally terrifying.

Not... vulnerable. *Hurt.*

Because of something Alexander had done.

"I'm sorry," he said, and folded her into his arms.

She was stiff for a moment, then wrapped her arms around him and held on tight.

"I never intended my behavior to reflect badly

on you," he told her. "And I know good intentions won't bring your friends back. I'm sorry. I'll do better."

"Or not," Belle said. "It depends what you think is 'better.' Repairing your reputation or following your heart."

$\mathcal{C}$ ynthia Louise took a long, steaming hot
bath in silence.

What was there to say? Although her bedchamber was down the corridor from the entranceway, the door had been left open and she'd
heard every word.

The crowd was loud enough, she'd likely have
heard it all even if the door was locked tight and
her head was buried under her pillow.

Alexander still planned to select a bride from
his young, pretty guests.

That had *always* been the plan. Cynthia knew
that. It was the reason she and Gertie were here.

And yet, confirmation that he had not wavered
in this mission stung as sharp as the arrow wound
in her shoulder.

"I'll help with your shift and gown," Gertie
offered.

Cynthia nodded her appreciation.

They picked a violet frock with oversized
puffed sleeves, in order to hide the wound from
delicate sensibilities. She covered the stitches with

a thick square of gauze, and tied it loosely in place with a strip of dark cloth, to mask any blood that might escape.

It looked like a badly placed mourning arm band.

That was also how she felt. Out of place, with her chest empty inside.

"Shall I ask the footmen to look for the skis?" Gertie asked.

"No," Cynthia answered. "The merrymaking is over."

Even the Christmastide party was falling apart.

"It looked like you and Nottingvale *were* enjoying yourselves," Gertie said tentatively. "Before I barged in."

"Oh, Gertie, it's not *your* fault." Cynthia wrapped her cousin in a one-armed embrace. "It's not anyone's fault. It's the way of the world. He's a duke. I'm me. We should never have been together, even for stolen moments. We knew we were playing with fire."

She'd never expected him to acknowledge their... friendship.

He'd never planned for such a contingency either.

That their affiliation was now public knowledge brought no joy or pride. The only reason his interest wasn't still a secret he planned to carry to the grave was because she'd taken an arrow to the shoulder.

Huzzah.

Acknowledged.

And in doing so, she'd ruined his plans... and possibly his life.

Now he wasn't the Perfect Duke of Nottingvale anymore. That myth had shattered the moment he dove down a mountain to gather her in his arms— when he was supposed to be courting *respectable* ladies at his house party.

His mother was right.

Cynthia was demonstrably bad for him.

If she liked him at all, the kindest thing she could do was leave him alone.

As she should have done from the beginning.

"He should have married you," Cynthia told Gertie.

Gertie shook her head. "I didn't want him to."

"You should have done so anyway." Cynthia sighed. "Gertie, at this point... I don't see how we're going to find you an alternate match capable of appeasing your father. We've less than a week. I can't go anywhere until these stitches heal a little, not that my presence would help you even if I did."

"Nottingvale isn't the only man at the party," Gertie said. "I had a lovely chat with Timmy Wilson while we were waiting for the duchess to summon tea. He'll be eighteen in six months. Timmy is new to archery, but he's very good at—"

"Gertie," Cynthia interrupted. "*No.*"

Her cousin's shoulders sagged, and she looked suddenly much older than her eighteen years.

"I know." Gertie's lips twisted in a sad smile. "This was my last chance to pretend."

Cynthia kissed her forehead. "Come on. There's a party out there. Mayhap there's a gentleman or two you'd do well to meet."

"What about you?" Gertie asked. "Did you ever consider any of the gentlemen?"

Yes.

There was one.

With soft brown hair and warm brown eyes and a kiss that could melt the snow from a mountaintop.

"No," she said firmly.

Gertie's eyes were sympathetic. "Are you in love with him?"

No.

Yes.

Damn it all!

"No," Cynthia said even more firmly.

Or it *would* have been firm, if the word hadn't wobbled coming out of her throat, only to audibly crack at the very end.

She blinked hard and pasted on a smile. "It's time to meet the ladies for Speculation. You remember how to count the cards, don't you?"

A knock sounded on the door.

Cynthia and Gertie exchanged glances.

"Did you ring the bell pull?" Cynthia whispered.

Gertie shook her head and whispered back, "It could be Doctor Quinney."

"And it might not be," Cynthia pointed out.

The knock came again.

She rolled back her shoulders and immediately regretted it. Pain shot through her as though the arrow had struck again.

Gritting her teeth against the injury, she wrenched open the door.

It was Alexander.

"I won't come in," he began.

"You're not invited in," she told him.

"But this needs to be said." He took a deep breath as if gathering courage, then met her eyes. "Although you are not what I'm looking for in a duchess, I cannot deny I enjoy your company. Marrying you will cause even more scandal on top of the unfortunate revelations that occurred today, but by refraining from unbecoming conduct in the future, with time and assiduous effort, I can rebuild some of my lost reputation."

Cynthia stared at him. "What?"

"For now, the damage has been done," he said. "My primary concern is the future. Heirs will need to be raised to be respectable pillars. There can be no further embarrassments to the title or the family. I'm sure you understand."

"I think I do understand," she said. "Now that there's a smudge on your sheen and the debutantes you *actually* wanted won't have you, you've decided to save your reputation by turning our compromising situation into a surprise betrothal... on condition that I become an entirely different person."

"Yes," he said. "Exactly. It'll save your reputation, too. You'll be important and watched carefully, but I'm certain you can—"

"I'm certain I *cannot*," Cynthia said flatly. "This isn't a marriage proposal. It's a script for a performance. You're not trying to be 'husband and wife' but rather 'duke and duchess.'"

"I *am* a duke," he told her. "My wife *will* be a duchess."

"But that shouldn't be *all* she is, or all that *you* are. Can't a duchess also be her own person, too?"

His jaw tightened. "Not if she brings shame to—"

"Let me stop you there. Don't try to 'save' me. Save your own reputation by not worrying about mine." She flashed a teeth-baring smile. "It will apparently shock you to discover that I don't *want* a husband who's ashamed of me. If you're too embarrassed to be seen with me, go and find a bride you can stand."

She slammed the door in his face, then sagged her good shoulder against it.

Gertie winced in sympathy. "That went well?"

Cynthia stumbled forward and dropped her forehead onto her cousin's shoulder. "That was a disaster. I'm a disaster. The only man to ask for my hand led with, 'You're an embarrassment. I'm ashamed to acknowledge you publicly, but since we've been thoroughly compromised, the precious *rules* force my hand...'"

"You choose to be a disaster," Gertie pointed out. "You could follow the rules if you wished to."

"I *don't* wish to." Cynthia lifted her head. "I couldn't be what he wants, no matter how hard I tried. He wants perfection. I'm... me."

"You are perfect," Gertie said. "I love you exactly as you are. And you're right. So would your husband... in a love match."

"Oh, Gertie." Cynthia scrubbed her face. "Am I being selfish? None of the women in that parlor are hoping to be chosen because of an emotional connection. It's like a game of whist. Some cards outrank others. Some hands are *better* than others. It's not personal. I shouldn't take it that way. It's just a game."

"No," Gertie said. "I cannot think of anything more personal than choosing the person you intend to spend the rest of your life with. You're not selfish to want a husband who is pleased to have married you. You're the bravest person I know. You'd rather have a partner than a title, and you're not afraid to stand up to a duke."

"He wasn't even *trying* to 'win' me," Cynthia said. "I don't want to be the thing he settles for only because I'm what Fate saddled him with. I'd rather be alone than unhappily married to the man I love."

"So you are in love," Gertie said softly.

Cynthia swallowed hard. "And now I'll watch him pick someone else."

CHAPTER 14

*A*lexander tried to make small talk.

All of his conversations felt smaller by the hour.

He couldn't stop thinking about Cynthia Louise.

She had spent the past three days taking meals in her room. Alexander had spent the past three days with the rest of his party, pretending to feel festive.

He wanted to give her a chance to heal without being plagued by guests, or... *him.*

He wanted to give her so much more than that.

But she had emphatically declined his offer to marry, and she was right to do so.

Mother had been appalled to learn that Alexander had suggested the union. She had been delighted that at least Cynthia Louise had the good sense not to make a bad situation worse.

So why did Alexander feel like *this* was the worst?

He was standing in an extravagant ballroom decorated with bright ribbons and boughs of holly. He was surrounded by a slightly diminished but still impressive number of sweet, pretty, well bred, respectable, proper young ladies who would *not* slam a door in his face if he offered to make her his duchess.

But he didn't want to.

They were all perfectly fine. They were *better* than fine. Each of them were splendid, accomplished women who would be a credit to the title and no doubt caring mothers to their future children.

But they weren't Cynthia Louise.

He shouldn't care.

It shouldn't matter.

He hadn't planned this party intending to marry her in the first place. As she'd rightfully pointed out, he would not have offered if extraordinary circumstances hadn't divulged his indiscretion. He should be thrilled she hadn't taken him up on his offer.

Thrilled.

Squeals filled the ballroom as the blindfolded gentleman with outstretched arms in the center almost touched one of the other guests before they could dance away, laughing.

It was as though Alexander were at a completely different party.

"Your Grace!" A rosy-cheeked miss held up a long strip of cloth. "Do you want a turn?"

"No, thank you," he called back, pressing himself deeper into the wainscoting.

He didn't need a blindfold.

Alexander was adept at avoiding uncomfortable truths.

Such as, his offer to Cynthia Louise had been no better than the morning seventeen-year-old Alexander Borland had woken up the new Duke of Nottingvale.

Here's a coronet. Now, be someone else.

Alexander hadn't been given a choice. Primogeniture forced the change upon him. He'd gone from an adolescent lad to a powerful lord overnight.

The rules had saved him.

Those same rules would stifle Cynthia.

Asking her to *not be* all of the things he liked best about her... What kind of offer was that?

A duchess had expectations she was required to live up to. He should choose someone who *wanted* to live by the strictures of the beau monde. Who would thrive ruling that world, not wither within it.

If he liked Cynthia, he should leave her be.

His sister Belle emerged from the crowd and joined him against the wall. "Not playing the game?"

"There's no way to win," he muttered.

His heart was torn in two.

The thought of living without Cynthia Louise was infinitely worse than the scandal of choosing her.

But he was a duke, and duty came first.

"How is Cynthia Louise?" his sister asked.

"I haven't seen her."

"Whose fault is that?"

He sent her a flat stare.

She blinked innocently and turned her gaze back to the ballroom. "Skis, eh? Was it terrifying?"

"Yes," he replied. "And the most amusing afternoon I ever had... Until it wasn't."

"Mm." She made a moue. "Mother says you narrowly avoided leg-shackling yourself to a mortifying hoyden."

Said like that, it sounded horrid.

Said like that, Mother's words resembled Alexander's speech to Cynthia Louise.

"I asked," he told his sister. "She declined."

Belle raised her brows. "*Did* you ask? Or did you imperiously inform her of your ducal decision?"

He glared at her. "What's the difference?"

Belle's eyes widened and she shook her head. "If you have to ask, then I have my answer."

"We don't suit," he said.

Belle's expression was suspiciously blank. "Mm-hm."

"The weight of this title almost crushed me. I cannot ask Cynthia Louise to voluntarily subject herself to the same fate."

"You definitely didn't ask," Belle murmured. "From the sounds of it."

"She doesn't have to be a duchess," he told his sister. "Cynthia can be and do anything she pleases."

Belle nodded. "Like marry a man who appreciates her just as she is."

Jealousy roared through Alexander's veins, hot and thick and itchy. He could not stand the thought of some other man with Cynthia Louise. Juggling chestnuts with her, sliding down mountains with her, *loving* her.

It was Alexander who—

"Oh, *bollocks*," he muttered.

He loved her.

That was the *reason* he'd gone sliding down a mountain, the first time as well as the second.

It wasn't the skis.

It was Cynthia.

Belle brightened considerably. "Something wrong, dear brother?"

He closed his eyes and leaned the back of his head against the wall. "The doctor's diagnosis was right."

Alexander had fallen in love.

And there was nothing he could do about it.

"If I could be so bold," Belle began.

"Please don't," he growled.

"You've probably been an absolute mutton-head," she continued.

He glared at her. "Dukes aren't muttonheads."

"Perhaps not *all* dukes," she said meaningfully.

Sisters were the worst.

"It's all right not to be perfect," she said.

"It's literally my duty to be as perfect as possible."

"And it's all right to *admit* when you haven't been perfect. Not to me," she added quickly. "To the person who most needs to hear it."

"What good would it do?"

"It would show her who you are," Belle said softly. "Isn't that who you really wanted her to accept?"

A marriage was between husband and wife, Cynthia had said.

Not duke and duchess.

Those were the posts they would hold, not the

people they were inside.

"Follow your heart," Belle said. "Not the 'rules.'"

"Society—" he began.

"—will not be standing at the altar," Belle finished.

He sighed. "Our mother—"

"—is also not the one choosing a bride." Belle touched his arm. "*You* are. Who you marry is up to you."

Except it wasn't.

He had asked.

Cynthia said no.

Alexander glared at the merry revelers in his ballroom.

He'd had enough of the party. Making it through tonight's dancing would be trial enough. He couldn't stand another minute of joyful festivities.

"If you'll excuse me," he murmured to his sister.

He managed to take three entire strides out of the ballroom before he ran into the next person likely to be brimming with unsolicited advice on how best to live his life.

"Mother," he said politely.

"Where are you going? The party is in there," she hissed. "You haven't an assignation with that Finch creature, do you?"

"She has a name," he replied coolly. "You're to call her 'Miss Finch' unless she gives you leave to do otherwise."

"Oh, for the love of..." The duchess pinched her lips. "Be *glad* she refused you. Can you imagine what a lifetime of marriage to her would be like?"

"I've been imagining it without cease for the

past three days," he replied. "I think I have a fairly clear idea."

"Good," his mother snapped, though her brow was furrowed. "You were raised to do the right thing, Vale."

He inclined his head. "And I shall do it."

Before his mother could waylay him with more reminders of endless responsibilities, he bowed and strode off down the corridor in the direction of the guest chambers.

As he and Cynthia had climbed back up the incline after their first trip down the mountain, she had confessed the untenable future awaiting Lady Gertrude.

He knew just how to remedy the situation.

It would involve dancing.

He knocked on their door.

After a brief pause, Lady Gertrude answered it.

Cynthia Louise was in an armchair before the window, her back to him.

She did not turn around.

"You recall my intention to select my bride by inviting her to be the first to dance at the farewell Twelfth Night ball?"

Lady Gertrude stared up at him in wide-eyed silence.

"There's no need to tarry. I've made my decision. I request your company at tonight's ball. Both of you. Please be present by eight o'clock."

Cynthia's back was still to him.

Lady Gertrude's eyes had only gone wider.

"Wear your dancing slippers," he ordered, and shut the door before either woman could do so for him.

CHAPTER 15

"Well," said Cynthia Louise, "at least one thing turned out for the best."

"No." Gertie blanched. "You can't make me."

Cynthia sighed. "You're right. I cannot make you marry Nottingvale. But if you don't, your father can and will force you to marry a man much, much worse."

"But Nottingvale is yours!" Gertie protested.

"He's not mine. He never *wanted* to be mine. He has moved on, and so must we."

Gertie crossed her arms.

Cynthia arched a brow.

Gertie made an aggravated sound. "Why would he do this?"

Cynthia turned to the wardrobe.

"For the same reason he does everything," she said. "To do the 'right thing.'"

Alexander was exactly the type of duke who would marry a debutante he didn't love because her good blood and impeccable reputation would bring honor to his title.

He was also exactly the type of man who would pick Gertie above all of the other perfectly perfect young ladies, because Cynthia had mentioned Gertie needed saving, and Alexander was the sort to try and save someone else, at any cost to himself.

That was what his obsession with "duty" was about:

Saving.

He wanted to save the standings and reputations of his title, his mother, his sister, his future heirs. He wanted to save face. He wanted to save himself from spectacle, from being seen as anything less than proper.

And now he wanted to save Gertie.

"You could do much worse," Cynthia said. "He's clever, he's kind, he's handsome... He'll provide for you with everything in his power. He doesn't know how to do anything else. Once you're his, he'll protect you to the ends of the earth. You're very..."

Lucky.

She rooted through the wardrobe to hide her face from Gertie. When she collected herself, Cynthia selected the fanciest gown, and handed it to her cousin.

"Put this on."

This time, Gertie didn't argue.

Cynthia helped dress her in silence.

Gertie was exactly what Alexander was looking for. This was exactly the outcome they'd come in hopes of achieving. Everyone had won.

Huzzah.

"You don't have to pretend to like this," Gertie said softly.

Cynthia's eyes stung with sudden heat. She was glad Gertie couldn't see her while she laced her cousin's gown.

"I ruined his plans and his party and he wasn't even courting me," Cynthia said. "Just imagine if we were married."

Just imagine.

It took all her strength to keep the image from her mind.

"Why did you decide to be unmarriageable?" Gertie asked.

"That's not what I decided," Cynthia said. "When I realized everyone else already thought that, I decided to do as I pleased. If I'm going to be alone with myself for the rest of my life, I might as well enjoy it. Polite Society rejected me, so I reject them."

"What if you could have both?" Gertie asked. "What if you could be part of Society *and* enjoy your life?"

"I *can't* have both." Cynthia's voice cracked. "I tried. I was the picture of propriety until my twenty-fourth birthday. I was such a pathetic wall-flower at assemblies, even *I* forgot I was there. When I decided to the devil with my reputation, do you know what happened?"

"You lost your Almack's subscription?"

"Besides that." Cynthia tied the ribbon and tucked the excess in a hidden panel. "People remembered me. I had *fun*. I made *friends*. Perhaps not the crowd I'd been raised to covet, but I can go out dancing every night for a year if I wish, and the only danger will be blisters on my feet rather than bunions on my behind."

Gertie whipped around. "One cannot develop bunions on one's derrière!"

"*You've* never spent seven straight hours straight perched on one of Almack's spinster chairs. Losing my voucher was the best thing that could have happened to my derrière."

"But did you want to lose it?" Gertie asked. "Or did you hope you could be yourself and still be accepted?"

Cynthia smiled sadly. "Does it matter?"

"I think it does." Gertie's forehead lined. "If your reaction to their disapproval was to become England's greatest hoyden for the sake of *im*propriety, then aren't you doing the same thing as before?"

Cynthia took a step backward. "It's the opposite of before."

Gertie shook her head. "All you've done is switch out one set of rules for another. Whatever you 'shouldn't' say, you say. Whatever you 'shouldn't' do, you do. You're as bound to your bad reputation as Nottingvale is to his good one."

Cynthia stared at her cousin in consternation.

Gertie was right.

Cynthia *had* exchanged one set of rules for another. She'd nurtured her "naughty scamp" reputation as armor against a Polite Society that had been anything but polite to a shy young woman yearning for acceptance.

Being "bad" felt good. It gave her power. It let her believe that she didn't need them, just like they didn't need her. It made her think she was free.

When, in fact, everything she did was *still* dictated by how it would look to the people who had ignored her.

"You don't have to prove anything," Gertie said. "Being Cynthia Louise is enough."

It had never been enough.

Not for Society.

Not for Alexander.

Not even for Cynthia herself.

Some people just weren't meant to be chosen for themselves.

"Come along," she said briskly. "It's almost eight o'clock, and the handsome prince awaits."

Gertie hesitated. "Are you going to wear... that?"

Cynthia glanced down at her comfortable, if wrinkled, day dress and shrugged.

"No one will see me," she reminded Gertie. "I'll be behind the pianoforte the entire time."

Gertie frowned. "What about your stitches?"

"They're healed enough. I don't even need the gauze anymore. Besides, do you think I'll allow some other spinster to play the betrothal waltz for my baby cousin?"

The ballroom was packed with people.

Word had already spread that tonight was the night the Duke of Nottingvale would choose his future duchess from the crowd of primped and perfect debutantes, each of them blushing prettily with excitement.

Despite her bravado, Cynthia *did* regret her wrinkled gown. Even at her best, she could not compare with these sparkling diamonds. Just the sight of them was enough to reduce her back to the naïve, hopeful wallflower she'd once been.

She tugged at her skirts and seated herself at the pianoforte before too many eyes could turn in her direction. Gertie hovered protectively at her side.

A hush fell over the room.

The Duke of Nottingvale had entered.

Cynthia could tell where he was by the turning of heads and the feminine gasps of swooning approval.

And then there he was.

Spotless black boots, breeches that showed his strong legs to perfection, gorgeous waistcoat the orange-red of autumn leaves, perfectly tailored coat of coal black superfine, a boyish tumble of wavy brown hair above warm brown eyes and all-too-kissable lips...

It was time.

Gertie was going to be a bride.

"Cynthia Louise?" he said.

"Without delay," she said quickly. Cynthia nudged Gertie toward the dance floor and positioned her fingers over the keys.

"Your cousin is a lovely, charming woman," began the Duke of Nottingvale.

Cynthia nodded without looking up. She could play this waltz. She *could*.

"But her name isn't 'Cynthia Louise,'" he finished.

Her fingers fell limply against the keys, bleating out a discordant jumble into the preternatural stillness of the ballroom.

She snatched her hands from the ivory and jerked her gaze toward his.

He stepped onto the dais.

She stared at him.

When he reached the pianoforte, he knelt on one knee beside her.

She tried to breathe.

"Cynthia Louise Finch," he said softly. "I choose *you*."

She definitely couldn't breathe.

"There is only one rule that matters." He took her hands in his. "My life means nothing without you in it."

She almost toppled from the bench.

"I botched the proposal the first time." His warm thumbs stroked her trembling hands. "I pray it's not too late to prove to you how much you mean to me."

"Your reputation," she stammered.

"Does not matter as much to me as you do."

"But propriety..." Her pulse fluttered so fast, her heart felt like a bird struggling against its cage. "The beau monde's rules and expectations..."

"Can take a flying leap from a snowy mountain." His eyes held hers.

She felt dizzy. Could he really mean it?

"Before," he said, "I was scared of losing my reputation. Now, the only thing that frightens me is the thought of losing you."

She gripped his hands tight and pressed them to her bosom.

"Miss Finch is... stealing Christmas!" came the disgruntled harrumph of a chaperone.

"You can have Christmas," the duke called over

his shoulder. His eyes met Cynthia's. "Miss Finch has my heart."

He pulled her to her feet and kept her hands in his.

"I'm scared too," she admitted. "What if I can't be what you want me to be?"

"I want you to be you," he said. "And I warn you, this means being burdened with *me*."

There would be no escaping Polite Society.

Alexander was a duke, and she would be a duchess, and their heirs would be lords and ladies. Cynthia would not only have to abide by *some* rules, but also teach them to her children.

Not to smother them with expectations, but to give them tools to make wise decisions for themselves.

"I can try my best," she told him. "But I won't be perfect."

"I hope I won't be, either." He gave her a crooked smile. "I thought we might meet somewhere in the middle."

"I would like that very much."

He pulled her away from the pianoforte to the middle of the dais.

The crowd pressed closer, as though holding their collective breaths.

"I've learned life isn't about following arbitrary rules." He touched her cheek. "It's about recognizing when you've met the right person, and creating your own rules together."

She tilted her face into his palm.

"*So romantic*," breathed one of the debutantes, before swooning into her mother's arms.

Cynthia felt the same.

"Being a duchess doesn't mean you must stop being you." He smoothed a tendril behind her ear. "I love you, Cynthia Louise Finch. For exactly who you are. You helped me find joy again. Do you think you might one day come to love me, too?"

Her heart hammered.

"I love you already, you impossible man," she choked out. "I loved you when we were playing billiards, and I loved you when we took our spontaneous tour of the castle, and I loved you when we flew down a mountain together on skis. I also love you for being such a wonderful brother to Belle, and for starting a fashion venture for the less fortunate, and for all of your work in the House of Lords. I love *you*, Alexander. I love *all* of you."

"In that case..." He glanced at their wide-eyed audience, then turned back to Cynthia with a slow grin. "May I have this dance?"

She nodded jerkily.

He lifted his gaze over her shoulder. "Lady Gertrude, would you do the honors?"

"Straight away," came Gertie's gleeful voice. "What shall I play?"

Alexander's expression turned mischievous. "Do you happen to know the timeless classic, 'A Spinster Goes A-Wenching?'"

Cynthia burst out laughing.

"Of course I do," said Gertie. "Everything worth knowing, I learned from Cynthia Louise."

The ballroom filled with the lively melody.

"Cynthia Louise Finch," said the Duke of Nottingvale. "Will you marry me?"

"Of course I will." She gave him a wicked grin

of her own. "Even if it means I have to create new lyrics for the song."

He pulled her into his arms. "This time, we can create our song together."

And they began to dance.

EPILOGUE

Twelfth Night

The farewell ball was underway, and the ballroom overflowed with revelers.

A few mothers and daughters had departed the festivities early, but the rest of the party stayed to enjoy Christmastide. This had certainly become one to remember.

Once news broke of Cynthia and Alexander's betrothal, the poor butler had been forced to prop the front door open to allow in the endless streams of gawkers and well-wishers.

Alexander had appeared in a gossip column!

The Duke of Nottingvale was scandalously in love with his new betrothed, and it was simply *not done*.

All of their friends in the village of Cressmouth delighted in their obvious affection for one another, and toasted the new couple at every opportunity.

The dowager duchess would have to make her peace with the new arrangement, as would Gertie's father.

Alexander had declared himself Gertie's new sponsor.

He had no legal claim to his new relative, but he outranked her father and was putting all of his influence behind Gertie to give her not only as much time as she desired to choose her future husband when she was ready, but also was arranging for the best music tutors in Europe, as well as opportunities for her to perform her pieces professionally.

Gertie was ecstatic at her new fortune, and could not be pried away from the pianoforte even by the bouncing, barking antics of a newly healed, boisterous Max.

Max, for his part, thrilled to be cooed over and played with by hundreds of new friends, both inside the house and out. One of the guests had apparently invented a new game, involving a dozen lords leaping through the rear garden, tossing sticks for Max to fetch.

"What is he going to do tomorrow?" Cynthia asked her soon-to-be husband. "When all of the guests leave?"

Alexander wiggled his eyebrows suggestively. "A better question is, what are *we* going to do tomorrow, once all of our guests leave?"

"Rock climbing?" she suggested innocently. "I thought we could toss a rope out of the castle's topmost tower, and descend the stones from the outside using our fingers. And then, *after* breakfast—"

"Mm, how I would *love* to risk my neck for no reason at all. Unfortunately, the doctor was very clear, darling. You must rest. In *bed*."

"That was last week," she reminded him. "My stitches are gone."

"Try it my way once," he suggested. "And then if you still prefer to jump out of a tower attached to a rope, I'll go with you."

"Excellent parry. I accept your offer of bed-chamber adventures."

"I'll make certain you don't regret it."

They never did return to the castle tower.

～

AUTHOR'S NOTE

*I*s "Cousin Olaf" a *Frozen* reference? Well, he can be, but Olaf was also very real!

Olaf Rye was born in 1791, which makes him a few years younger than Cynthia Louise. Olaf was born in Norway, died in Denmark, and had a celebrated military career.

More importantly to our story, he holds a ski jumping world record!

On 22 November, 1808, in Eidsberg, Norway, he did indeed launch himself 10 yards / 9.5 meters in the air, as described in *Forever Your Duke*.

Our story takes place six years later, which means his historic jump coincides with the moment when Cynthia Louise decided to stop being a wallflower and start being the heroine of her own life.

What a way to begin!

xoxo,

Erica

THANK YOU FOR READING

Love talking books with fellow readers?

Join the *Historical Romance Book Club* for prizes, books, and live chats with your favorite romance authors:
Facebook.com/groups/HistRomBookClub

And check out the official website for sneak peeks and more:
www.EricaRidley.com/books

THE DUKE HEIST

WILD WYNCHESTERS #1

A secret identities, class divide romance from a *New York Times* bestselling author: Why seduce a duke the normal way, when you can accidentally kidnap one in an elaborately planned heist?

Chloe Wynchester is completely forgettable -- a curse that gives her the ability to blend into any crowd. When the only father she's ever known makes a dying wish for his adopted family of orphans to recover a missing painting, she's the first one her siblings turn to for stealing it back. No one expects that in doing so, she'll also abduct a handsome duke.

Lawrence Gosling, the Duke of Faircliffe, is tortured by his father's mistakes. To repair his estate's ruined reputation, he must wed a highborn heiress. Yet when he finds himself in a carriage being driven hell-for-leather down the cobblestone streets of London by a beautiful woman who refuses to heed his commands, he fears his heart is hers. But how can he sacrifice his family's legacy to follow true love?

"Erica Ridley is a delight!"
　—Julia Quinn

"Irresistible romance and a family of delightful scoundrels... I want to be a Wynchester!"
　—Eloisa James

ABOUT THE AUTHOR

Erica Ridley is a *New York Times* and *USA Today* best-selling author of witty, feel-good historical romance novels, including the upcoming THE DUKE HEIST, featuring the Wild Wynchesters. Why seduce a duke the normal way, when you can accidentally kidnap one in an elaborately planned heist?

In the *12 Dukes of Christmas* series, enjoy witty, heartwarming Regency romps nestled in a picturesque snow-covered village. After all, nothing heats up a winter night quite like finding oneself in the arms of a duke!

Two popular series, the *Dukes of War* and *Rogues to Riches*, feature roguish peers and dashing war heroes who find love amongst the splendor and madness of Regency England.

When not reading or writing romances, Erica can be found riding camels in Africa, zip-lining through rainforests in Central America, or getting hopelessly lost in the middle of Budapest.

~

Let's be friends! Find Erica on:
www.EricaRidley.com

CPSIA information can be obtained
at www.ICGtesting.com
Printed in the USA
LVHW112037100521
687025LV00001B/14